John Greenleaf Whittier

Legends and Lyrics from the Poetic Works..

John Greenleaf Whittier

Legends and Lyrics from the Poetic Works..

ISBN/EAN: 9783744782814

Printed in Europe, USA, Canada, Australia, Japan

Cover: Foto ©Andreas Hilbeck / pixelio.de

More available books at **www.hansebooks.com**

LEGENDS AND LYRICS

FROM THE POETIC WORKS OF JOHN GREENLEAF WHITTIER

BOSTON AND NEW YORK
HOUGHTON, MIFFLIN AND COMPANY
The Riverside Press, Cambridge
M DCCC XC

THE TENT ON THE BEACH.

. . . .

And one there was, a dreamer born,
   Who, with a mission to fulfil,
Had left the Muses' haunts to turn
   The crank of an opinion-mill,
Making his rustic reed of song
A weapon in the war with wrong,
Yoking his fancy to the breaking-plough
That beam-deep turned the soil for truth to
      spring and grow.

Too quiet seemed the man to ride
   The wingéd Hippogriff Reform ;
Was his a voice from side to side
   To pierce the tumult of the storm ?
A silent, shy, peace-loving man,
He seemed no fiery partisan
To hold his way against the public frown,
The ban of Church and State, the fierce mob's
      hounding down.

For while he wrought with strenuous will
   The work his hands had found to do,
He heard the fitful music still
   Of winds that out of dream-land blew.

The din about him could not drown
What the strange voices whispered down ;
Along his task-field weird processions swept,
The visionary pomp of stately phantoms stepped.

The common air was thick with dreams, —
He told them to the toiling crowd ;
Such music as the woods and streams
Sang in his ear he sang aloud ;
In still, shut bays, on windy capes,
He heard the call of beckoning shapes,
And, as the gray old shadows prompted him,
To homely moulds of rhyme he shaped their legends
grim.

.   .   .   .

CONTENTS.

6 *Contents.*

LEGENDS AND LYRICS.

THE ANGELS OF BUENA VISTA.

SPEAK and tell us, our Ximena,
     looking northward far away,
     O'er the camp of the invaders,
     o'er the Mexican array,
Who is losing? who is winning? are they
     far or come they near?
Look abroad, and tell us, sister, whither
     rolls the storm we hear.

"Down the hills of Angostura still the
     storm of battle rolls;
Blood is flowing, men are dying; God
     have mercy on their souls!"
Who is losing? who is winning? "Over
     hill and over plain,
I see but smoke of cannon clouding
     through the mountain rain."

Holy Mother ! keep our brothers ! Look,
    Ximena, look once more.
" Still I see the fearful whirlwind rolling
    darkly as before,
Bearing on, in strange confusion, friend
    and foeman, foot and horse,
Like some wild and troubled torrent
    sweeping down its mountain
    course."

Look forth once more, Ximena ! " Ah !
    the smoke has rolled away ;
And I see the Northern rifles gleaming
    down the ranks of gray.
Hark ! that sudden blast of bugles ! there
    the troop of Minon wheels ;
There the Northern horses thunder, with
    the cannon at their heels.

" Jesu, pity ! how it thickens ! now re-
    treat and now advance !
Right against the blazing cannon shivers
    Puebla's charging lance !
Down they go, the brave young riders ;
    horse and foot together fall ;
Like a ploughshare in the fallow, through
    them ploughs the Northern ball."

Nearer came the storm and nearer, rolling
    fast and frightful on !
Speak, Ximena, speak and tell us, who
    has lost, and who has won ?
" Alas ! alas ! I know not ; friend and foe
    together fall,
O'er the dying rush the living : pray, my
    sisters, for them all !

"Lo ! the wind the smoke is lifting.
    Blessed Mother, save my brain !
I can see the wounded crawling slowly
    out from heaps of slain.
Now they stagger, blind and bleeding ;
    now they fall, and strive to rise ;
Hasten, sisters, haste and save them, lest
    they die before our eyes !

"O my heart's love ! O my dear one !
    lay thy poor head on my knee ;
Dost thou know the lips that kiss thee ?
    Canst thou hear me ? canst thou
    see ?
O my husband, brave and gentle ! O my
    Bernal, look once more
On the blessed cross before thee ! Mercy !
    mercy ! all is o'er ! "

Dry thy tears, my poor Ximena; lay thy
    dear one down to rest;
Let his hands be meekly folded, lay the
    cross upon his breast;
Let his dirge be sung hereafter, and his
    funeral masses said;
To-day, thou poor bereaved one, the liv-
    ing ask thy aid.

Close beside her, faintly moaning, fair and
    young, a soldier lay,
Torn with shot and pierced with lances,
    bleeding slow his life away;
But, as tenderly before him the lorn Xi-
    mena knelt,
She saw the Northern eagle shining on his
    pistol-belt.

With a stifled cry of horror straight she
    turned away her head;
With a sad and bitter feeling looked she
    back upon her dead;
But she heard the youth's low moaning,
    and his struggling breath of pain,
And she raised the cooling water to his
    parching lips again.

Whispered low the dying soldier, pressed
    her hand and faintly smiled;
Was that pitying face his mother's? did
    she watch beside her child?
All his stranger words with meaning her
    woman's heart supplied;
With her kiss upon his forehead, " Mo-
    ther!" murmured he, and died!

" A bitter curse upon them, poor boy, who
    led thee forth,
From some gentle, sad-eyed mother, weep-
    ing, lonely, in the North!"
Spake the mournful Mexic woman, as she
    laid him with her dead,
And turned to soothe the living, and bind
    the wounds which bled.

Look forth once more, Ximena! "Like
    a cloud before the wind
Rolls the battle down the mountains, leav-
    ing blood and death behind;
Ah! they plead in vain for mercy; in the
    dust the wounded strive;
Hide your faces, holy angels! O thou
    Christ of God, forgive!"

Sink, O Night, among thy mountains ! let
 the cool, gray shadows fall ;
Dying brothers, fighting demons, drop thy
 curtain over all !
Through the thickening winter twilight,
 wide apart the battle rolled,
In its sheath the sabre rested, and the
 cannon's lips grew cold.

But the noble Mexic women still their
 holy task pursued,
Through that long, dark night of sorrow,
 worn and faint and lacking food.
Over weak and suffering brothers, with a
 tender care they hung,
And the dying foeman blessed them in a
 strange and Northern tongue.

Not wholly lost, O Father ! is this evil
 world of ours ;
Upward, through its blood and ashes,
 spring afresh the Eden flowers ;
From its smoking hell of battle, Love and
 Pity send their prayer,
And still thy white-winged angels hover
 dimly in our air !

HAMPTON BEACH.

THE sunlight glitters keen and bright,
  Where miles away,
 Lies stretching to my dazzled sight
 A luminous belt, a misty light,
Beyond the dark pine bluffs and wastes of
  sandy gray.

 The tremulous shadow of the Sea !
  Against its ground
 Of silvery light, rock, hill, and tree,
 Still as a picture, clear and free,
With varying outline mark the coast for
  miles around.

 On — on — we tread with loose-flung
  rein
  Our seaward way,
 Through dark-green fields and blossom-
  ing grain,
 Where the wild brier-rose skirts the
  lane,
And bends above our heads the flowering
  locust spray.

Ha ! like a kind hand on my brow
    Comes this fresh breeze,
Cooling its dull and feverish glow,
While through my being seems to flow
The breath of a new life, the healing of
    the seas !

Now rest we, where this grassy mound
    His feet hath set
In the great waters, which have bound
His granite ankles greenly round
With long and tangled moss, and weeds
    with cool spray wet.

Good-by to Pain and Care ! I take
    Mine ease to-day :
Here where these sunny waters break,
And ripples this keen breeze, I shake
All burdens from the heart, all weary
    thoughts away.

I draw a freer breath, I seem
    Like all I see —
Waves in the sun, the white - winged
    gleam
Of sea-birds in the slanting beam,
And far-off sails which flit before the
    south-wind free.

So when Time's veil shall fall asunder,
　　The soul may know
No fearful change, nor sudden wonder,
Nor sink the weight of mystery under,
But with the upward rise, and with the
　　vastness grow.

And all we shrink from now may seem
　　No new revealing ;
Familiar as our childhood's stream,
Or pleasant memory of a dream
The loved and cherished Past upon the
　　new life stealing.

Serene and mild the untried light
　　May have its dawning ;
And, as in summer's northern night
The evening and the dawn unite,
The sunset hues of Time blend with the
　　soul's new morning.

I sit alone ; in foam and spray
　　Wave after wave
Breaks on the rocks which, stern and
　　gray,
Shoulder the broken tide away,
Or murmurs hoarse and strong through
　　mossy cleft and cave.

What heed I of the dusty land
　　And noisy town?
I see the mighty deep expand
From its white line of glimmering sand
To where the blue of heaven on bluer
　　waves shuts down!

In listless quietude of mind,
　　I yield to all
The change of cloud and wave and
　　wind,
And passive on the flood reclined,
I wander with the waves, and with them
　　rise and fall.

But look, thou dreamer! wave and
　　shore
　　In shadow lie;
The night-wind warns me back once
　　more
To where, my native hill-tops o'er,
Bends like an arch of fire the glowing
　　sunset sky.

So then, beach, bluff, and wave, fare-
　　well!
　　I bear with me

No token stone nor glittering shell,
But long and oft shall Memory tell
Of this brief thoughtful hour of musing by
    the Sea.

ON RECEIVING AN EAGLE'S QUILL FROM LAKE SUPERIOR.

ALL day the darkness and the cold
    Upon my heart have lain,
    Like shadows on the winter sky,
    Like frost upon the pane ;

But now my torpid fancy wakes,
    And, on thy Eagle's plume,
Rides forth, like Sindbad on his bird,
    Or witch upon her broom !

Below me roar the rocking pines,
    Before me spreads the lake
Whose long and solemn-sounding waves
    Against the sunset break.

I hear the wild Rice-Eater thresh
  The grain he has not sown ;
I see, with flashing scythe of fire,
  The prairie harvest mown !

I hear the far-off voyager's horn ;
  I see the Yankee's trail, —
His foot on every mountain-pass,
  On every stream his sail.

By forest, lake, and waterfall,
  I see his pedler show ;
The mighty mingling with the mean,
  The lofty with the low.

He's whittling by St. Mary's Falls,
  Upon his loaded wain ;
He's measuring o'er the Pictured Rocks,
  With eager eyes of gain.

I hear the mattock in the mine,
  The axe-stroke in the dell,
The clamor from the Indian lodge,
  The Jesuit chapel bell !

I see the swarthy trappers come
  From Mississippi's springs ;

And war-chiefs with their painted brows,
    And crests of eagle wings.

Behind the scared squaw's birch canoe,
    The steamer smokes and raves ;
And city lots are staked for sale
    Above old Indian graves.

I hear the tread of pioneers
    Of nations yet to be ;
The first low wash of waves, where soon
    Shall roll a human sea.

The rudiments of empire here
    Are plastic yet and warm ;
The chaos of a mighty world
    Is rounding into form !

Each rude and jostling fragment soon
    Its fitting place shall find, —
The raw material of a State,
    Its muscle and its mind !

And, westering still, the star which leads
    The New World in its train
Has tipped with fire the icy spears
    Of many a mountain chain.

The snowy cones of Oregon
  Are kindling on its way ;
And California's golden sands
  Gleam brighter in its ray !

Then blessings on thy eagle quill,
  As, wandering far and wide,
I thank thee for this twilight dream
  And Fancy's airy ride !

Yet, welcomer than regal plumes,
  Which Western trappers find,
Thy free and pleasant thoughts, chance
      sown,
  Like feathers on the wind.

Thy symbol be the mountain-bird,
  Whose glistening quill I hold ;
Thy home the ample air of hope,
  And memory's sunset gold !

In thee, let joy with duty join,
  And strength unite with love,
The eagle's pinions folding round
  The warm heart of the dove !

So, when in darkness sleeps the vale
  Where still the blind bird clings,
The sunshine of the upper sky
  Shall glitter on thy wings !

TAULER.

TAULER, the preacher, walked,
    one autumn day,
    Without the walls of Strasburg,
  by the Rhine,
Pondering the solemn Miracle of Life ;
As one who, wandering in a starless night,
Feels momently the jar of unseen waves,
And hears the thunder of an unknown
    sea,
Breaking along an unimagined shore.

  And as he walked he prayed. Even
    the same
Old prayer with which, for half a score of
    years,
Morning, and noon, and evening, lip and
    heart

Had groaned : "Have pity upon me,
        Lord !
Thou seest, while teaching others, I am
        blind.
Send me a man who can direct my steps !"

    Then, as he mused, he heard along his
        path
A sound as of an old man's staff among
The dry, dead linden-leaves ; and, looking
        up,
He saw a stranger, weak, and poor, and
        old.

    " Peace be unto thee, father ! " Tauler
        said,
" God give thee a good day ! "   The old
        man raised
Slowly his calm blue eyes.   " I thank
        thee, son ;
But all my days are good, and none are
        ill."

Wondering thereat, the preacher spake
        again,
"God give thee happy life."   The old
        man smiled,
" I never am unhappy."

Tauler laid
His hand upon the stranger's coarse gray
    sleeve:
"Tell me, O father, what thy strange
    words mean.
Surely man's days are evil, and his life
Sad as the grave it leads to." " Nay, my
    son,
Our times are in God's hands, and all our
    days
Are as our needs ; for shadow as for sun,
For cold as heat, for want as wealth, alike
Our thanks are due, since that is best
    which is ;
And that which is not, sharing not His life,
Is evil only as devoid of good.
And for the happiness of which I spake,
I find it in submission to His will,
And calm trust in the holy Trinity
Of Knowledge, Goodness, and Almighty
    Power."

Silently wondering, for a little space,
Stood the great preacher ; then he spake
    as one
Who, suddenly grappling with a haunting
    thought

Which long has followed, whispering
    through the dark
Strange terrors, drags it, shrieking, into
    light:
"What if God's will consign thee hence
    to Hell?"

"Then," said the stranger, cheerily,
    "be it so.
What Hell may be I know not; this I
    know, —
I cannot lose the presence of the Lord.
One arm, Humility, takes hold upon
His dear Humanity; the other, Love,
Clasps his Divinity. So where I go
He goes; and better fire-walled Hell with
    Him
Than golden-gated Paradise without."

Tears sprang in Tauler's eyes. A sud-
    den light,
Like the first ray which fell on chaos,
    clove
Apart the shadow wherein he had walked
Darkly at noon. And, as the strange old
    man
Went his slow way, until his silver hair

Set like the white moon where the hills of
    vine
Slope to the Rhine, he bowed his head
    and said :
" My prayer is answered. God hath sent
    the man
Long sought, to teach me, by his simple
    trust,
Wisdom the weary schoolmen never
    knew."

    So, entering with a changed and cheer-
    ful step
The city gates, he saw, far down the street,
A mighty shadow break the light of noon,
Which tracing backward till its airy lines
Hardened to stony plinths, he raised his
    eyes
O'er broad façade and lofty pediment,
O'er architrave and frieze and sainted
    niche,
Up the stone lace-work chiselled by the
    wise
Erwin of Steinbach, dizzily up to where
In the noon-brightness the great Min-
    ster's tower,
Jewelled with sunbeams on its mural
    crown,

Rose like a visible prayer. " Behold ! "
    he said,
" The stranger's faith made plain before
    mine eyes.
As yonder tower outstretches to the earth
The dark triangle of its shade alone
When the clear day is shining on its top,
So, darkness in the pathway of Man's life
Is but the shadow of God's providence,
By the great Sun of Wisdom cast thereon ;
And what is dark below is light in
    Heaven."

THE BAREFOOT BOY.

BLESSINGS on thee, little man,
  Barefoot boy, with cheek of tan !
  With thy turned-up pantaloons,
And thy merry whistled tunes ;
With thy red lip, redder still
Kissed by strawberries on the hill ;
With the sunshine on thy face,
Through thy torn brim's jaunty grace ;

From my heart I give thee joy, —
I was once a barefoot boy!
Prince thou art, — the grown-up man
Only is republican.
Let the million-dollared ride!
Barefoot, trudging at his side,
Thou hast more than he can buy
In the reach of ear and eye, —
Outward sunshine, inward joy:
Blessings on thee, barefoot boy!

Oh, for boyhood's painless play,
Sleep that wakes in laughing day,
Health that mocks the doctor's rules,
Knowledge never learned of schools,
Of the wild bee's morning chase,
Of the wild-flower's time and place,
Flight of fowl and habitude
Of the tenants of the wood;
How the tortoise bears his shell,
How the woodchuck digs his cell,
And the ground-mole sinks his well;
How the robin feeds her young,
How the oriole's nest is hung;
Where the whitest lilies blow,
Where the freshest berries grow,
Where the ground-nut trails its vine,

Where the wood-grape's clusters shine ;
Of the black wasp's cunning way,
Mason of his walls of clay,
And the architectural plans
Of gray hornet artisans !
For, eschewing books and tasks,
Nature answers all he asks ;
Hand in hand with her he walks,
Face to face with her he talks,
Part and parcel of her joy, —
Blessings on the barefoot boy !

Oh, for boyhood's time of June,
Crowding years in one brief moon,
When all things I heard or saw,
Me, their master, waited for.
I was rich in flowers and trees,
Humming-birds and honey-bees ;
For my sport the squirrel played,
Plied the snouted mole his spade ;
For my taste the blackberry cone
Purpled over hedge and stone ;
Laughed the brook for my delight
Through the day and through the night,
Whispering at the garden wall,
Talked with me from fall to fall ;
Mine the sand-rimmed pickerel pond,

Mine the walnut slopes beyond,
Mine, on bending orchard trees,
Apples of Hesperides !
Still as my horizon grew,
Larger grew my riches too ;
All the world I saw or knew
Seemed a complex Chinese toy,
Fashioned for a barefoot boy !

Oh, for festal dainties spread,
Like my bowl of milk and bread ;
Pewter spoon and bowl of wood,
On the door-stone, gray and rude,
O'er me, like a regal tent,
Cloudy-ribbed, the sunset bent,
Purple-curtained, fringed with gold,
Looped in many a wind-swung fold ;
While for music came the play
Of the pied frogs orchestra ;
And, to light the noisy choir,
Lit the fly his lamp of fire.
I was monarch : pomp and joy
Waited on the barefoot boy !

Cheerily, then, my little man,
Live and laugh, as boyhood can !
Though the flinty slopes be hard,

Stubble-speared the new-mown sward,
Every morn shall lead thee through
Fresh baptisms of the dew;
Every evening from thy feet
Shall the cool wind kiss the heat:
All too soon these feet must hide
In the prison cells of pride,
Lose the freedom of the sod,
Like a colt's for work be shod,
Made to tread the mills of toil,
Up and down in ceaseless moil:
Happy if their track be found
Never on forbidden ground;
Happy if they sink not in
Quick and treacherous sands of sin.
Ah! that thou couldst know thy joy,
Ere it passes, barefoot boy!

THE KANSAS EMIGRANTS.

E cross the prairie as of old
    The pilgrims crossed the sea,
To make the West, as they the
    East,
The homestead of the free !

We go to rear a wall of men
    On Freedom's southern line,
And plant beside the cotton-tree
    The rugged Northern pine !

We 're flowing from our native hills
    As our free rivers flow ;
The blessing of our Mother-land
    Is on us as we go.

We go to plant her common schools
    On distant prairie swells,
And give the Sabbaths of the wild
    The music of her bells.

Upbearing, like the Ark of old,
    The Bible in our van,
We go to test the truth of God
    Against the fraud of man.

No pause, nor rest, save where the
    streams
  That feed the Kansas run,
Save where our Pilgrim gonfalon
    Shall flout the setting sun !

We 'll tread the prairie as of old
    Our fathers sailed the sea,
And make the West, as they the East,
    The homestead of the free !

MAUD MULLER.

AUD MULLER on a summer's
    day
    Raked the meadow sweet with
    hay.

Beneath her torn hat glowed the wealth
Of simple beauty and rustic health.

Singing, she wrought, and her merry glee
The mock-bird echoed from his tree.

But when she glanced to the far-off town,
White from its hill-slope looking down,

The sweet song died, and a vague unrest
And a nameless longing filled her
    breast, —

A wish, that she hardly dared to own,
For something better than she had known.

The Judge rode slowly down the lane,
Smoothing his horse's chestnut mane.

He drew his bridle in the shade
Of the apple-trees, to greet the maid,

And asked a draught from the spring that
    flowed
Through the meadow across the road.

She stooped where the cool spring bub-
    bled up,
And filled for him her small tin cup,

And blushed as she gave it, looking down
On her feet so bare, and her tattered
    gown.

"Thanks!" said the Judge; "a sweeter
        draught
From a fairer hand was never quaffed."

He spoke of the grass and flowers and
        trees,
Of the singing birds and the humming
        bees;

Then talked of the haying, and wondered
        whether
The cloud in the west would bring foul
        weather.

And Maud forgot her brier-torn gown,
And her graceful ankles bare and brown;

And listened, while a pleased surprise
Looked from her long-lashed hazel eyes.

At last, like one who for delay
Seeks a vain excuse, he rode away.

Maud Muller looked and sighed: "Ah
        me!
That I the Judge's bride might be!

" He would dress me up in silks so fine,
And praise and toast me at his wine.

" My father should wear a broadcloth coat ;
My brother should sail a painted boat.

" I 'd dress my mother so grand and gay,
And the baby should have a new toy each
    day.

" And I 'd feed the hungry and clothe the
    poor,
And all should bless me who left our
    door."

The Judge looked back as he climbed the
    hill,
And saw Maud Muller standing still.

" A form more fair, a face more sweet,
Ne'er hath it been my lot to meet.

" And her modest answer and graceful air
Show her wise and good as she is fair.

" Would she were mine, and I to-day,
Like her, a harvester of hay ;

" No doubtful balance of rights and
  wrongs,
Nor weary lawyers with endless tongues,

" But low of cattle and song of birds,
And health and quiet and loving words."

But he thought of his sisters, proud and
  cold,
And his mother, vain of her rank and
  gold.

So, closing his heart, the Judge rode on,
And Maud was left in the field alone.

But the lawyers smiled that afternoon,
When he hummed in court an old love-
  tune ;

And the young girl mused beside the well
Till the rain on the unraked clover fell.

He wedded a wife of richest dower,
Who lived for fashion, as he for power.

Yet oft, in his marble hearth's bright glow,
He watched a picture come and go ;

And sweet Maud Muller's hazel eyes
Looked out in their innocent surprise.

Oft, when the wine in his glass was red,
He longed for the wayside well instead;

And closed his eyes on his garnished
    rooms
To dream of meadows and clover-blooms.

And the proud man sighed, with a secret
    pain,
"Ah, that I were free again!

" Free as when I rode that day,
Where the barefoot maiden raked her hay."

She wedded a man unlearned and poor,
And many children played round her door.

But care and sorrow, and childbirth pain,
Left their traces on heart and brain.

And oft, when the summer sun shone hot
On the new-mown hay in the meadow lot,

And she heard the little spring brook fall
Over the roadside, through the wall,

In the shade of the apple-tree again
She saw a rider draw his rein.

And, gazing down with timid grace,
She felt his pleased eyes read her face.

Sometimes her narrow kitchen walls
Stretched away into stately halls ;

The weary wheel to a spinnet turned,
The tallow candle an astral burned,

And for him who sat by the chimney lug,
Dozing and grumbling o'er pipe and
        mug,

A manly form at her side she saw,
And joy was duty and love was law.

Then she took up her burden of life again,
Saying only, " It might have been."

Alas for maiden, alas for Judge,
For rich repiner and household drudge !

God pity them both ! and pity us all,
Who vainly the dreams of youth recall.

For of all sad words of tongue or pen,
The saddest are these : "It might have
    been ! "

Ah, well ! for us all some sweet hope lies
Deeply buried from human eyes ;

And, in the hereafter, angels may
Roll the stone from its grave away !

THE LAST WALK IN AUTUMN.

I.

'ER the bare woods, whose out-
    stretched hands
    Plead with the leaden heavens
    in vain,
I see, beyond the valley lands,
    The sea's long level dim with rain.
Around me all things, stark and dumb,
Seem praying for the snows to come,
And, for the summer bloom and greenness
    gone,
With winter's sunset lights and dazzling
    morn atone.

II.

Along the river's summer walk,
  The withered tufts of asters nod ;
And trembles on its arid stalk
  The hoar plume of the golden-rod.
And on a ground of sombre fir,
And azure-studded juniper,
The silver birch its buds of purple shows,
And scarlet berries tell where bloomed
    the sweet wild-rose !

III.

With mingled sound of horns and bells,
  A far-heard clang, the wild geese fly,
Storm-sent, from Arctic moors and fells,
  Like a great arrow through the sky,
Two dusky lines converged in one,
Chasing the southward-flying sun ;
While the brave snow-bird and the hardy
    jay
Call to them from the pines, as if to bid
    them stay.

IV.

I passed this way a year ago :
  The wind blew south; the noon of
    day

Was warm as June's; and save that
    snow
  Flecked the low mountains far away,
And that the vernal-seeming breeze
Mocked faded grass and leafless trees,
I might have dreamed of summer as I lay,
Watching the fallen leaves with the soft
    wind at play.

V.

Since then, the winter blasts have piled
  The white pagodas of the snow
On these rough slopes, and, strong and
    wild,
  Yon river, in its overflow
Of spring-time rain and sun, set free,
Crashed with its ices to the sea ;
And over these gray fields, then green and
    gold,
The summer corn has waved, the thun-
    der's organ rolled.

VI.

Rich gift of God ! A year of time !
  What pomp of rise and shut of day,
What hues wherewith our Northern
    clime

Makes autumn's dropping woodlands
gay,
What airs outblown from ferny dells,
And clover-bloom and sweetbrier smells,
What songs of brooks and birds, what
fruits and flowers,
Green woods and moonlit snows, have in
its round been ours !

VII.

I know not how, in other lands,
The changing seasons come and go ;
What splendors fall on Syrian sands,
What purple lights on Alpine snow !
Nor how the pomp of sunrise waits
On Venice at her watery gates ;
A dream alone to me is Arno's vale,
And the Alhambra's halls are but a trav-
eller's tale.

VIII.

Yet, on life's current, he who drifts
Is one with him who rows or sails ;
And he who wanders widest lifts
No more of beauty's jealous veils
Than he who from his doorway sees
The miracle of flowers and trees,

Feels the warm Orient in the noonday air,
And from cloud minarets hears the sunset
   call to prayer !

IX.

The eye may well be glad that looks
   Where Pharpar's fountains rise and
     fall ;
But he who sees his native brooks
   Laugh in the sun, has seen them all.
The marble palaces of Ind
Rise round him in the snow and wind ;
From his lone sweetbrier Persian Hafiz
   smiles,
And Rome's cathedral awe is in his wood-
   land aisles.

X.

And thus it is my fancy blends
   The near at hand and far and rare ;
And while the same horizon bends
   Above the silver-sprinkled hair
Which flashed the light of morning skies
On childhood's wonder-lifted eyes,
Within its round of sea and sky and field,
Earth wheels with all her zones, the Kos-
   mos stands revealed.

XI.

And thus the sick man on his bed,
　The toiler to his task-work bound,
Behold their prison-walls outspread,
　Their clipped horizon widen round!
While freedom-giving fancy waits,
Like Peter's angel at the gates,
The power is theirs to baffle care and pain,
To bring the lost world back, and make it
　　theirs again!

XII.

What lack of goodly company,
　When masters of the ancient lyre
Obey my call, and trace for me
　Their words of mingled tears and
　　fire!
I talk with Bacon, grave and wise,
I read the world with Pascal's eyes;
And priest and sage, with solemn brows
　　austere,
And poets, garland-bound, the Lords of
　　Thought, draw near.

XIII.

Methinks, O friend, I hear thee say,
　" In vain the human heart we mock;

Bring living guests who love the day,
    Not ghosts who fly at crow of cock !
The herbs we share with flesh and blood
Are better than ambrosial food
With laurelled shades."   I grant it, noth-
      ing loath,
But doubly blest is he who can partake of
      both.

XIV.

He who might Plato's banquet grace,
    Have I not seen before me sit,
And watched his puritanic face,
    With more than Eastern wisdom lit ?
Shrewd mystic ! who, upon the back
Of his Poor Richard's Almanac,
Writing the Sufi's song, the Gentoo's
      dream,
Links Manu's age of thought to Fulton's
      age of steam !

XV.

Here too, of answering love secure,
    Have I not welcomed to my hearth
The gentle pilgrim troubadour,
    Whose songs have girdled half the
      earth ;

Whose pages, like the magic mat
Whereon the Eastern lover sat,
Have borne me over Rhine-land's purple
    vines,
And Nubia's tawny sands, and Phrygia's
    mountain pines !

XVI.

And he, who to the lettered wealth
    Of ages adds the lore unpriced,
The wisdom and the moral health,
    The ethics of the school of Christ ;
The statesman to his holy trust,
As the Athenian archon, just,
Struck down, exiled like him for truth
    alone,
Has he not graced my home with beauty
    all his own ?

XVII.

What greetings smile, what farewells
    wave,
    What loved ones enter and depart !
The good, the beautiful, the brave,
    The Heaven-lent treasures of the
        heart !
How conscious seems the frozen sod

And beechen slope whereon they trod !
The oak-leaves rustle, and the dry grass
    bends
Beneath the shadowy feet of lost or ab-
    sent friends.

XVIII.

Then ask not why to these bleak hills
    I cling, as clings the tufted moss,
To bear the winter's lingering chills,
    The mocking spring's perpetual loss.
I dream of lands where summer smiles,
And soft winds blow from spicy isles,
But scarce would Ceylon's breath of flow-
    ers be sweet,
Could I not feel thy soil, New England,
    at my feet !

XIX.

At times I long for gentler skies,
    And bathe in dreams of softer air,
But homesick tears would fill the eyes
    That saw the Cross without the Bear.
The pine must whisper to the palm,
The north-wind break the tropic calm ;
And with the dreamy languor of the Line,
The North's keen virtue blend, and
    strength to beauty join.

XX.

Better to stem with heart and hand
The roaring tide of life, than lie,
Unmindful, on its flowery strand,
Of God's occasions drifting by !
Better with naked nerve to bear
The needles of this goading air,
Than, in the lap of sensual ease, forego
The godlike power to do, the godlike aim
to know.

XXI.

Home of my heart ! to me more fair
Than gay Versailles or Windsor's
halls,
The painted, shingly town-house where
The freeman's vote for Freedom
falls !
The simple roof where prayer is made,
Than Gothic groin and colonnade ;
The living temple of the heart of man,
Than Rome's sky-mocking vault, or many-
spired Milan !

XXII.

More dear thy equal village schools,
Where rich and poor the Bible read,

Than classic halls where Priestcraft
    rules,
  And Learning wears the chains of
    Creed ;
Thy glad Thanksgiving, gathering in
The scattered sheaves of home and kin,
Than the mad license ushering Lenten
    pains,
Or holidays of slaves who laugh and dance
    in chains.

XXIII.

And sweet homes nestle in these dales,
  And perch along these wooded swells ;
And, blest beyond Arcadian vales,
  They hear the sound of Sabbath bells !
Here dwells no perfect man sublime,
Nor woman winged before her time,
But with the faults and follies of the race,
Old home-bred virtues hold their not un-
    honored place.

XXIV.

Here manhood struggles for the sake
  Of mother, sister, daughter, wife,
The graces and the loves which make
  The music of the march of life ;

And woman, in her daily round
Of duty, walks on holy ground.
No unpaid menial tills the soil, nor here
Is the bad lesson learned at human rights
   to sneer.

XXV.

Then let the icy north-wind blow
   The trumpets of the coming storm,
To arrowy sleet and blinding snow
   Yon   slanting   lines   of   rain   trans-
      form.
Young hearts shall hail the drifted cold,
   As gayly as I did of old;
And I, who watch them through the frosty
      pane,
Unenvious, live in them my boyhood o'er
      again.

XXVI.

And I will trust that He who heeds
   The life that hides in mead and wold,
Who hangs yon alder's crimson beads,
   And stains these mosses green and
      gold,
Will still, as He hath done, incline
His gracious care to me and mine;

Grant what we ask aright, from wrong de-
    bar,
And, as the earth grows dark, make
    brighter every star !

XXVII.

I have not seen, I may not see,
    My hopes for man take form in
    fact,
But God will give the victory
    In due time ; in that faith I act.
And he who sees the future sure,
The baffling present may endure,
And bless, meanwhile, the unseen Hand
    that leads
The heart's desires beyond the halting
    step of deeds.

XXVIII.

And thou, my song, I send thee forth,
    Where harsher songs of mine have
    flown ;
Go, find a place at home and hearth
    Where'er thy singer's name is
    known ;
Revive for him the kindly thought
Of friends ; and they who love him not,

Touched by some strain of thine, perchance may take
The hand he proffers all, and thank him
 for thy sake.

THE GARRISON OF CAPE ANN.

ROM the hills of home forth look-
 ing far beneath the tent-like
 span
 Of the sky, I see the white gleam of the
  headland of Cape Ann.
Well I know its coves and beaches to the
 ebb-tide glimmering down,
And the white-walled hamlet children of
 its ancient fishing-town.

Long has passed the summer morning, and
 its memory waxes old,
When along yon breezy headlands with a
 pleasant friend I strolled.
Ah ! the autumn sun is shining, and the
 ocean wind blows cool,
And the golden-rod and aster bloom
 around thy grave, Rantoul !

With the memory of that morning by the
    summer sea I blend
A wild and wondrous story, by the
    younger Mather penned,
In that quaint *Magnalia Christi,* with all
    strange and marvellous things,
Heaped up huge and undigested, like the
    chaos Ovid sings.

Dear to me these far, faint glimpses of the
    dual life of old,
Inward, grand with awe and reverence;
    outward, mean and coarse and
    cold;
Gleams of mystic beauty playing over dull
    and vulgar clay,
Golden-threaded fancies weaving in a web
    of hodden gray.

The great eventful Present hides the Past;
    but through the din
Of its loud life hints and echoes from the
    life behind steal in;
And the lore of home and fireside, and the
    legendary rhyme,
Make the task of duty lighter which the
    true man owes his time.

So, with something of the feeling which
    the Covenanter knew,
When with pious chisel wandering Scot-
    land's   moorland   graveyards
    through,
From the graves of old traditions I part
    the blackberry-vines,
Wipe the moss from off the headstones,
    and retouch the faded lines.

Where the sea-waves back and forward,
    hoarse with rolling pebbles, ran,
The garrison-house stood watching on the
    gray rocks of Cape Ann ;
On its windy site uplifting gabled roof and
    palisade,
And rough walls of unhewn timber with
    the moonlight overlaid.

On his slow round walked the sentry,
    south and eastward looking forth
O'er a rude and broken coast-line, white
    with breakers stretching north, —
Wood and rock and gleaming sand-drift,
    jagged capes, with bush and tree,
Leaning inland from the smiting of the
    wild and gusty sea.

Before the deep-mouthed chimney, dimly
    lit by dying brands,
Twenty soldiers sat and waited, with their
    muskets in their hands;
On the rough-hewn oaken table the veni-
    son haunch was shared,
And the pewter tankard circled slowly
    round from beard to beard.

Long they sat and talked together, —
    talked of wizards Satan-sold;
Of all ghostly sights and noises, — signs
    and wonders manifold;
Of the spectre-ship of Salem, with the
    dead men in her shrouds,
Sailing sheer above the water, in the loom
    of morning clouds;

Of the marvellous valley hidden in the
    depths of Gloucester woods,
Full of plants that love the summer, —
    blooms of warmer latitudes;
Where the Arctic birch is braided by the
    tropic's flowery vines,
And the white magnolia-blossoms star the
    twilight of the pines!

But their voices sank yet lower, sank to
    husky tones of fear,
As they spake of present tokens of the
    powers of evil near ;
Of a spectral host, defying stroke of steel
    and aim of gun ;
Never yet was ball to slay them in the
    mould of mortals run !

Thrice, with plumes and flowing scalp-
    locks, from the midnight wood they
    came, —
Thrice around the block-house marching,
    met, unharmed, its volleyed flame ;
Then, with mocking laugh and gesture,
    sunk in earth or lost in air,
All the ghostly wonder vanished, and the
    moonlit sands lay bare.

Midnight came ; from out the forest
    moved a dusky mass that soon
Grew to warriors, plumed and painted,
    grimly marching in the moon.
" Ghosts or witches," said the captain,
    " thus I foil the Evil One ! "
And he rammed a silver button, from his
    doublet, down his gun.

Once again the spectral horror moved the
  guarded wall about;
Once again the levelled muskets through
  the palisades flashed out,
With that deadly aim the squirrel on his
  tree-top might not shun,
Nor the beach-bird seaward flying with his
  slant wing to the sun.

Like the idle rain of summer sped the
  harmless shower of lead.
With a laugh of fierce derision, once again
  the phantoms fled ;
Once again, without a shadow on the sands
  the moonlight lay,
And the white smoke curling through it
  drifted slowly down the bay !

"God preserve us !" said the captain;
  " never mortal foes were there ;
They have vanished with their leader
  Prince and Power of the air !
Lay aside your useless weapons; skill
  and prowess naught avail ;
They who do the Devil's service wear
  their master's coat of mail !"

So the night grew near to cock-crow, when
    again a warning call
Roused the score of weary soldiers watch-
    ing round the dusky hall :
And they looked to flint and priming, and
    they longed for break of day ;
But the captain closed his Bible : " Let us
    cease from man, and pray ! "

To the men who went before us, all the
    unseen powers seemed near,
And their steadfast strength of courage
    struck its roots in holy fear.
Every hand forsook the musket, every
    head was bowed and bare,
Every stout knee pressed the flag-stones,
    as the captain led in prayer.

Ceased thereat the mystic marching of the
    spectres round the wall,
But a sound abhorred, unearthly, smote
    the ears and hearts of all, —
Howls of rage and shrieks of anguish !
    Never after mortal man
Saw the ghostly leaguers marching round
    the block-house of Cape Ann.

So to us who walk in summer through the
    cool and sea-blown town,
From the childhood of its people comes
    the solemn legend down.
Not in vain the ancient fiction, in whose
    moral lives the youth
And the fitness and the freshness of an
    undecaying truth.

Soon or late to all our dwellings come the
    spectres of the mind,
Doubts and fears and dread forebodings,
    in the darkness undefined ;
Round us throng the grim projections of
    the heart and of the brain,
And our pride of strength is weakness,
    and the cunning hand is vain.

In the dark we cry like children ; and no
    answer from on high
Breaks the crystal spheres of silence, and
    no white wings downward fly ;
But the heavenly help we pray for comes
    to faith, and not to sight,
And our prayers themselves drive back-
    ward all the spirits of the night !

THE GIFT OF TRITEMIUS.

RITEMIUS of Herbipolis, one day,
  While kneeling at the altar's foot
    to pray,
Alone with God, as was his pious choice,
Heard from without a miserable voice,
A sound which seemed of all sad things
    to tell,
As of a lost soul crying out of hell.

Thereat the Abbot paused; the chain
    whereby
His thoughts went upward broken by that
    cry;
And, looking from the casement, saw be-
    low
A wretched woman, with gray hair a-flow,
And withered hands held up to him, who
    cried
For alms as one who might not be denied.

She cried, " For the dear love of Him who
    gave

His life for ours, my child from bondage
save, —
My beautiful, brave first-born, chained
with slaves
In the Moor's galley, where the sun-smit
waves
Lap the white walls of Tunis ! " — " What
I can
I give," Tritemius said, " my prayers." —
" O man
Of God ! " she cried, for grief had made
her bold,
" Mock me not thus ; I ask not prayers,
but gold.
Words will not serve me, alms alone
suffice ;
Even while I speak perchance my first-
born dies."

" Woman ! " Tritemius answered, " from
our door
None go unfed, hence are we always
poor ;
A single soldo is our only store.
Thou hast our prayers ; — what can we
give thee more ? "

"Give me," she said, "the silver candle-
　　sticks
On either side of the great crucifix.
God well may spare them on His errands
　　sped,
Or He can give you golden ones instead."

Then spake Tritemius, "Even as thy word,
Woman, so be it! (Our most gracious
　　Lord,
Who loveth mercy more than sacrifice,
Pardon me if a human soul I prize
Above the gifts upon his altar piled!)
Take what thou askest, and redeem thy
　　child."

But his hand trembled as the holy alms
He placed within the beggar's eager
　　palms ;
And as she vanished down the linden
　　shade,
He bowed his head and for forgiveness
　　prayed.

So the day passed, and when the twilight
　　came
He woke to find the chapel all aflame,

And, dumb with grateful wonder, to be-
    hold
Upon the altar candlesticks of gold !

SKIPPER IRESON'S RIDE.

F all the rides since the birth of
    time,
    Told in story or sung in rhyme, —
On Apuleius's Golden Ass,
Or one-eyed Calendar's horse of brass,
Witch astride of a human back,
Islam's prophet on Al-Borák, —
The strangest ride that ever was sped
Was Ireson's out from Marblehead !
  Old Floyd Ireson, for his hard heart,
  Tarred and feathered and carried in a
    cart
    By the women of Marblehead !

Body of turkey, head of owl,
Wings a-droop like a rained-on fowl,

Feathered and ruffled in every part,
Skipper Ireson stood in the cart.
Scores of women, old and young,
Strong of muscle, and glib of tongue,
Pushed and pulled up the rocky lane,
Shouting and singing the shrill refrain :
  "Here's Flud Oirson, fur his horrd
        horrt,
  Torr'd an' futherr'd an' corr'd in a corrt
  By the women o' Morble'ead ! "

Wrinkled scolds with hands on hips,
Girls in bloom of cheek and lips,
Wild-eyed, free-limbed, such as chase
Bacchus round some antique vase,
Brief of skirt, with ankles bare,
Loose of kerchief and loose of hair,
With conch-shells blowing and fish-horns'
        twang,
Over and over the Mænads sang :
  "Here's Flud Oirson, fur his horrd
        horrt,
  Torr'd an' futherr'd an' corr'd in a corrt
  By the women o' Morble'ead ! "

Small pity for him ! — He sailed away
From a leaking ship, in Chaleur Bay, —

Sailed away from a sinking wreck,
With his own town's-people on her deck !
"Lay by ! lay by !" they called to him.
Back he answered, "Sink or swim !
Brag of your catch of fish again !"
And off he sailed through the fog and
    rain !
    Old Floyd Ireson, for his hard heart,
    Tarred and feathered and carried in a
      cart
    By the women of Marblehead !

Fathoms deep in dark Chaleur
That wreck shall lie forevermore.
Mother and sister, wife and maid,
Looked from the rocks of Marblehead
Over the moaning and rainy sea, —
Looked for the coming that might not be !
What did the winds and the sea-birds say
Of the cruel captain who sailed away ? —
    Old Floyd Ireson, for his hard heart,
    Tarred and feathered and carried in a
      cart
    By the women of Marblehead !

Through the street, on either side,
Up flew windows, doors swung wide ;

Sharp-tongued spinsters, old wives gray,
Treble lent the fish-horn's bray.
Sea-worn grandsires, cripple-bound,
Hulks of old sailors run aground,
Shook   head,   and   fist,   and   hat,   and
    cane,
And cracked with curses the hoarse re-
    frain :
    " Here 's Flud Oirson, fur his horrd
        horrt,
    Torr'd an' futherr'd an' corr'd in a corrt
      By the women o' Morble'ead !

Sweetly along the Salem road
Bloom of orchard and lilac showed.
Little the wicked skipper knew
Of the fields so green and the sky so
    blue.
Riding there in his sorry trim,
Like an Indian idol glum and grim,
Scarcely he seemed the sound to hear
Of voices shouting, far and near :
    " Here 's Flud Oirson, fur his horrd
        horrt,
    Torr'd an' futherr'd an' corr'd in a
      corrt
      By the women o' Morble'ead ! "

" Hear me, neighbors ! " at last he cried ? —
" What to me is this noisy ride ?
What is the shame that clothes the skin
To the nameless horror that lives within ?
Waking or sleeping, I see a wreck,
And hear a cry from a reeling deck !
Hate me and curse me, — I only dread
The hand of God and the face of the
    dead ! "
    Said old Floyd Ireson, for his hard
      heart,
    Tarred and feathered and carried in a
      cart
    By the women of Marblehead !

Then the wife of the skipper lost at sea
Said, " God has touched him ! why should
    we ? "
Said an old wife mourning her only son,
" Cut the rogue's tether and let him run ! "
So with soft relentings and rude excuse,
Half scorn, half pity, they cut him loose,
And gave him a cloak to hide him in,
And left him alone with his shame and sin.
    Poor Floyd Ireson, for his hard heart,
    Tarred and feathered and carried in a
      cart
    By the women of Marblehead !

TELLING THE BEES.

HERE is the place; right over the hill
    Runs the path I took;
You can see the gap in the old wall still,
    And the stepping-stones in the shallow
        brook.

There is the house, with the gate red-
        barred
    And the poplars tall;
And the barn's brown length, and the cat-
        tle-yard,
    And the white horns tossing above the
        wall.

There are the beehives ranged in the sun;
    And down by the brink
Of the brook are her poor flowers, weed-
        o'errun,
    Pansy and daffodil, rose and pink.

A year has gone, as the tortoise goes,
    Heavy and slow;
And the same rose blows, and the same
        sun glows,
    And the same brook sings of a year ago.

There's the same sweet clover-smell in
 the breeze ;
 And the June sun warm
Tangles his wings of fire in the trees,
 Setting, as then, over Fernside farm.

I mind me how with a lover's care
 From my Sunday coat
I brushed off the burrs, and smoothed my
 hair,
 And cooled at the brookside my brow
 and throat.

Since we parted, a month had passed, —
 To love, a year ;
Down through the beeches I looked at
 last
 On the little red gate and the well-sweep
 near.

I can see it all now, — the slantwise rain
 Of light through the leaves,
The sundown's blaze on her window-pane,
 The bloom of her roses under the eaves.

Just the same as a month before, —
 The house and the trees,

The barn's brown gable, the vine by the
    door, —
  Nothing changed but the hives of
    bees.

Before them, under the garden wall,
    Forward and back,
Went drearily singing the chore-girl small,
  Draping each hive with a shred of black.

Trembling I listened : the summer sun
    Had the chill of snow ;
For I knew she was telling the bees of
    one
  Gone on the journey we all must go !

Then I said to myself, "My Mary weeps
    For the dead to-day :
Haply her blind old grandsire sleeps
  The fret and the pain of his age away."

But her dog whined low ; on the doorway
    sill,
  With his cane to his chin,
The old man sat ; and the chore - girl
    still
  Sung to the bees stealing out and in.

And the song she was singing ever
since
In my ear sounds on : —
" Stay at home, pretty bees, fly not hence !
Mistress Mary is dead and gone ! "

THE SWAN SONG OF PARSON AVERY.

WHEN the reaper's task was ended,
and the summer wearing late,
Parson Avery sailed from Newbury, with his wife and children eight,
Dropping down the river-harbor in the
shallop " Watch and Wait."

Pleasantly lay the clearings in the mellow
summer-morn,
With the newly planted orchards dropping
their fruits first-born,
And the home-roofs like brown islands
amid a sea of corn.

Broad meadows reached out seaward the
    tided creeks between,
And hills rolled wave-like inland, with
    oaks and walnuts green ; —
A fairer home, a goodlier land, his eyes
    had never seen.

Yet away sailed Parson Avery, away where
    duty led,
And the voice of God seemed calling, to
    break the living bread
To the souls of fishers starving on the
    rocks of Marblehead.

All day they sailed : at nightfall the pleas-
    ant land-breeze died,
The blackening sky, at midnight, its starry
    lights denied,
And far and low the thunder of tempest
    prophesied !

Blotted out were all the coast-lines, gone
    were rock, and wood, and sand ;
Grimly anxious stood the skipper with the
    rudder in his hand,
And questioned of the darkness what was
    sea and what was land.

And the preacher heard his dear ones,
    nestled round him, weeping sore :
" Never heed, my little children ! Christ
    is walking on before
To the pleasant land of heaven, where the
    sea shall be no more."

All at once the great cloud parted, like a
    curtain drawn aside,
To let down the torch of lightning on the
    terror far and wide ;
And the thunder and the whirlwind to-
    gether smote the tide.

There was wailing in the shallop, woman's
    wail and man's despair,
A crash of breaking timbers on the rocks
    so sharp and bare,
And, through it all, the murmur of Father
    Avery's prayer.

From his struggle in the darkness with the
    wild waves and the blast,
On a rock, where every billow broke
    above him as it passed,
Alone, of all his household, the man of
    God was cast.

There a comrade heard him praying, in
    the pause of wave and wind:
"All my own have gone before me, and I
    linger just behind;
Not for life I ask, but only for the rest
    Thy ransomed find!

"In this night of death I challenge the
    promise of Thy word! —
Let me see the great salvation of which
    mine ears have heard! —
Let me pass from hence forgiven, through
    the grace of Christ, our Lord!

"In the baptism of these waters wash
    white my every sin,
And let me follow up to Thee my house-
    hold and my kin!
Open the sea-gate of Thy heaven, and let
    me enter in!"

When the Christian sings his death-song,
    all the listening heavens draw near,
And the angels, leaning over the walls of
    crystal, hear
How the notes so faint and broken swell to
    music in God's ear.

The ear of God was open to His servant's
    last request ;
As the strong wave swept him downward
    the sweet hymn upward pressed,
And the soul of Father Avery went, sing-
    ing, to its rest.

There was wailing on the mainland, from
    the rocks of Marblehead ;
In the stricken church of Newbury the
    notes of prayer were read ;
And long, by board and hearthstone, the
    living mourned the dead.

And still the fishers outbound, or scud-
    ding from the squall,
With grave and reverent faces, the an-
    cient tale recall,
When they see the white waves breaking
    on the Rock of Avery's Fall !

THE DOUBLE-HEADED SNAKE OF NEW-BURY.

" Concerning yᵉ Amphisbæna, as soon as I received your commands, I made diligent inquiry : . . . . he assures me yᵗ it had really two heads, one at each end ; two mouths, two stings or tongues." — REV. CHRISTOPHER TOPPAN *to* COTTON MATHER.

AR away in the twilight time
　　Of every people, in every clime,
　　Dragons and griffins and mon-
　　　　sters dire,
Born of water, and air, and fire,
Or nursed, like the Python, in the mud
And ooze of the old Deucalion flood,
Crawl and wriggle and foam with rage,
Through dusk tradition and ballad age.
So from the childhood of Newbury town
And its time of fable the tale comes down
Of a terror which haunted bush and brake,
The Amphisbæna, the Double Snake !

Thou who makest the tale thy mirth,
Consider that strip of Christian earth
On the desolate shore of a sailless sea,
Full of terror and mystery,
Half redeemed from the evil hold
Of the wood so dreary, and dark, and old,

Which drank with its lips of leaves the dew
When Time was young, and the world was
    new,
And wove its shadows with sun and moon,
Ere the stones of Cheops were squared
    and hewn.
Think of the sea's dread monotone,
Of the mournful wail from the pine-wood
    blown,
Of the strange, vast splendors that lit the
    North,
Of the troubled throes of the quaking
    earth,
And the dismal tales the Indian told,
Till the settler's heart at his hearth grew
    cold,
And he shrank from the tawny wizard
    boasts,
And the hovering shadows seemed full of
    ghosts,
And above, below, and on every side,
The fear of his creed seemed verified ; —
And think, if his lot were now thine own,
To grope with terrors nor named nor
    known,
How laxer muscle and weaker nerve
And a feebler faith thy need might serve ;

And own to thyself the wonder more
That the snake had two heads, and not a
  score!

Whether he lurked in the Oldtown fen
Or the gray earth - flax of the Devil's
  Den,
Or swam in the wooded Artichoke,
Or coiled by the Northman's Written
  Rock,
Nothing on record is left to show;
Only the fact that he lived, we know,
And left the cast of a double head
In the scaly mask which he yearly shed.
For he carried a head where his tail should
  be,
And the two, of course, could never agree,
But wriggled about with main and might,
Now to the left and now to the right;
Pulling and twisting this way and that,
Neither knew what the other was at.

A snake with two heads, lurking so near!
Judge of the wonder, guess at the fear!
Think what ancient gossips might say,
Shaking their heads in their dreary way,
Between the meetings on Sabbath-day!

How urchins, searching at day's decline
The Common Pasture for sheep or kine,
The terrible double-ganger heard
In leafy rustle or whir of bird !
Think what a zest it gave to the sport,
In berry-time, of the younger sort,
As over pastures blackberry-twined,
Reuben and Dorothy lagged behind,
And closer and closer, for fear of harm,
The maiden clung to her lover's arm ;
And how the spark, who was forced to
    stay,
By his sweetheart's fears, till the break of
    day,
Thanked the snake for the fond delay !

Far and wide the tale was told,
Like a snowball growing while it rolled.
The nurse hushed with it the baby's
    cry ;
And it served, in the worthy minister's
    eye,
To paint the primitive serpent by.
Cotton Mather came galloping down
All the way to Newbury town,
With his eyes agog and his ears set wide,
And his marvellous inkhorn at his side ;

Stirring the while in the shallow pool
Of his brains for the lore he learned at
    school,
To garnish the story, with here a streak
Of Latin, and there another of Greek :
And the tales he heard and the notes he
    took,
Behold ! are they not in his Wonder-Book?

Stories, like dragons, are hard to kill.
If the snake does not, the tale runs still
In Byfield Meadows, on Pipestave Hill.
And still, whenever husband and wife
Publish the shame of their daily strife,
And, with mad cross-purpose, tug and
    strain
At either end of the marriage-chain,
The gossips say, with a knowing shake
Of their gray heads, "Look at the Double
    Snake !
One in body and two in will,
The Amphisbæna is living still ! "

MABEL MARTIN.

A HARVEST IDYL.

PROEM.

CALL the old time back : I
bring my lay
In tender memory of the summer day
When, where our native river lapsed away,

We dreamed it over, while the thrushes
made
Songs of their own, and the great pine-
trees laid
On warm moonlights the masses of their
shade.

And *she* was with us, living o'er again
Her life in ours, despite of years and
pain, —
The Autumn's brightness after latter rain.

Beautiful in her holy peace as one
Who stands, at evening, when the work is
done,
Glorified in the setting of the sun !

Her memory makes our common land-
    scape seem
Fairer than any of which painters dream ;
Lights the brown hills and sings in every
    stream ;

For she whose speech was always truth's
    pure gold
Heard, not unpleased, its simple legends
    told,
And loved with us the beautiful and old.

I. THE RIVER VALLEY.

Across the level tableland,
   A grassy, rarely trodden way,
   With thinnest skirt of birchen spray

And stunted growth of cedar, leads
   To where you see the dull plain fall
   Sheer off, steep-slanted, ploughed by
    all

The seasons' rainfalls. On its brink
   The over-leaning harebells swing,
   With roots half bare the pine-trees
    cling ;

And, through the shadow looking west,
　　You see the wavering river flow
　　Along a vale, that far below

Holds to the sun, the sheltering hills
　　And glimmering water-line between,
　　Broad fields of corn and meadows green,

And fruit-bent orchards grouped around
　　The low brown roofs and painted eaves,
　　And chimney-tops half hid in leaves.

No warmer valley hides behind
　　Yon wind - scourged sand - dunes, cold
　　　　and bleak ;
　　No fairer river comes to seek

The wave-sung welcome of the sea,
　　Or mark the northmost border line
　　Of sun-loved growths of nut and vine.

Here, ground-fast in their native fields,
　　Untempted by the city's gain,
　　The quiet farmer folk remain

Who bear the pleasant name of Friends,
　　And keep their fathers' gentle ways
　　And simple speech of Bible days ;

In whose neat homesteads woman holds
  With modest ease her equal place,
  And wears upon her tranquil face

The look of one who, merging not
  Her self-hood in another's will,
  Is love's and duty's handmaid still.

Pass with me down the path that winds
  Through birches to the open land,
  Where, close upon the river strand,

You mark a cellar, vine o'errun,
  Above whose wall of loosened stones
  The sumach lifts its reddening cones,

And the black nightshade's berries shine,
  And broad, unsightly burdocks fold
  The household ruin, century-old.

Here, in the dim colonial time
  Of sterner lives and gloomier faith,
  A woman lived, tradition saith,

Who wrought her neighbors foul annoy,
  And witched and plagued the country-
      side,
  Till at the hangman's hand she died.

Sit with me while the westering day
  Falls slantwise down the quiet vale,
  And, haply ere you loitering sail,

That rounds the upper headland, falls
  Below Deer Island's pines, or sees
  Behind it Hawkswood's belt of trees

Rise black against the sinking sun,
  My idyl of its days of old,
  The valley's legend, shall be told.

II. THE HUSKING.

It was the pleasant harvest-time,
  When cellar-bins are closely stowed,
  And garrets bend beneath their load,

And the old swallow-haunted barns, —
  Brown-gabled, long, and full of seams
  Through which the moted sunlight
    streams,

And winds blow freshly in, to shake
  The red plumes of the roosted cocks,
  And the loose hay-mow's scented
    locks, —

Are filled with summer's ripened stores,
  Its odorous grass and barley sheaves,
  From their low scaffolds to their
    eaves.

On Esek Harden's oaken floor,
  With many an autumn threshing worn,
  Lay the heaped ears of unhusked
    corn.

And thither came young men and maids,
  Beneath a moon that, large and low,
  Lit that sweet eve of long ago.

They took their places ; some by chance,
  And others by a merry voice
  Or sweet smile guided to their choice.

How pleasantly the rising moon,
  Between the shadow of the mows,
  Looked on them through the great elm-
    boughs !

On sturdy boyhood, sun-embrowned,
  On girlhood with its solid curves
  Of healthful strength and painless
    nerves !

And jests went round, and laughs that
    made
  The house - dog answer with his
    howl,
  And kept astir the barn-yard fowl ;

And quaint old songs their fathers
    sung
  In Derby dales and Yorkshire moors,
  Ere Norman William trod their shores ;

And tales, whose merry license shook
  The fat sides of the Saxon thane,
  Forgetful of the hovering Dane, —

Rude plays to Celt and Cimbri known,
  The charms and riddles that beguiled
  On Oxus' banks the young world's
    child, —

That primal picture-speech wherein
  Have youth and maid the story told,
  So new in each, so dateless old,

Recalling pastoral Ruth in her
  Who waited, blushing and demure,
  The red-ear's kiss of forfeiture.

III. THE WITCH'S DAUGHTER.

But still the sweetest voice was mute
 That river-valley ever heard
 From lips of maid or throat of bird ;

For Mabel Martin sat apart,
 And let the hay-mow's shadow fall
 Upon the loveliest face of all.

She sat apart, as one forbid,
 Who knew that none would condescend
 To own the Witch-wife's child a friend.

The seasons scarce had gone their round,
 Since curious thousands thronged to see
 Her mother at the gallows-tree ;

And mocked the prison-palsied limbs
 That faltered on the fatal stairs,
 And wan lip trembling with its prayers !

Few questioned of the sorrowing child,
 Or, when they saw the mother die,
 Dreamed of the daughter's agony.

They went up to their homes that day,
 As men and Christians justified :
 God willed it, and the wretch had died !

Dear God and Father of us all,
    Forgive our faith in cruel lies, —
    Forgive the blindness that denies!

Forgive Thy creature when he takes,
    For the all-perfect love Thou art,
    Some grim creation of his heart.

Cast down our idols, overturn
    Our bloody altars ; let us see
    Thyself in Thy humanity!

Young Mabel from her mother's grave
    Crept to her desolate hearth-stone,
    And wrestled with her fate alone ;

With love, and anger, and despair,
    The phantoms of disordered sense,
    The awful doubts of Providence!

Oh, dreary broke the winter days,
    And dreary fell the winter nights
    When, one by one, the neighboring lights

Went out, and human sounds grew still,
    And all the phantom-peopled dark
    Closed round her hearth - fire's dying
        spark.

And summer days were sad and long,
  And sad the uncompanioned eves,
  And sadder sunset-tinted leaves,

And Indian Summer's airs of balm ;
  She scarcely felt the soft caress,
  The beauty died of loneliness !

The school-boys jeered her as they passed
  And, when she sought the house of
      prayer,
  Her mother's curse pursued her there.

And still o'er many a neighboring door
  She saw the horseshoe's curvëd charm,
  To guard against her mother's harm :

That mother, poor and sick and lame,
  Who daily, by the old arm-chair,
  Folded her withered hands in prayer ; —

Who turned, in Salem's dreary jail,
  Her worn old Bible o'er and o'er,
  When her dim eyes could read no more !

Sore tried and pained, the poor girl kept
  Her faith, and trusted that her way,
  So dark, would somewhere meet the day.

And still her weary wheel went round
Day after day, with no relief:
Small leisure have the poor for grief.

IV. THE CHAMPION.

So in the shadow Mabel sits;
Untouched by mirth she sees and
hears,
Her smile is sadder than her tears.

But cruel eyes have found her out,
And cruel lips repeat her name,
And taunt her with her mother's
shame.

She answered not with railing words,
But drew her apron o'er her face,
And, sobbing, glided from the place.

And only pausing at the door,
Her sad eyes met the troubled gaze
Of one who, in her better days,

Had been her warm and steady friend,
Ere yet her mother's doom had made
Even Esek Harden half afraid.

He felt that mute appeal of tears,
  And, starting, with an angry frown,
  Hushed all the wicked murmurs down.

" Good neighbors mine," he sternly said,
  "This passes harmless mirth or jest ;
  I brook no insult to my guest.

" She is indeed her mother's child ;
  But God's sweet pity ministers
  Unto no whiter soul than hers.

" Let Goody Martin rest in peace ;
  I never knew her harm a fly,
  And witch or not, God knows, — not I.

" I know who swore her life away ;
  And as God lives, I 'd not condemn
  An Indian dog on word of them."

The broadest lands in all the town,
  The skill to guide, the power to awe,
  Were Harden's ; and his word was law.

None dared withstand him to his face,
  But one sly maiden spake aside :
  " The little witch is evil-eyed !

" Her mother only killed a cow,
    Or witched a churn or dairy-pan ;
    But she, forsooth, must charm a man ! "

V. IN THE SHADOW.

Poor Mabel, homeward turning, passed
    The nameless terrors of the wood,
    And saw, as if a ghost pursued,

Her shadow gliding in the moon ;
    The soft breath of the west-wind
        gave
    A chill as from her mother's grave.

How dreary seemed the silent house !
    Wide in the moonbeams' ghastly glare
    Its windows had a dead man's stare !

And, like a gaunt and spectral hand,
    The tremulous shadow of a birch
    Reached out and touched the door's low
        porch,

As if to lift its latch ; hard by,
    A sudden warning call she heard,
    The night-cry of a boding bird.

She leaned against the door ; her face,
   So fair, so young, so full of pain,
   White in the moonlight's silver rain.

The river, on its pebbled rim,
   Made music such as childhood knew ;
   The door - yard tree was whispered
      through

By voices such as childhood's ear
   Had heard in moonlights long ago ;
   And through the willow-boughs below

She saw the rippled waters shine ;
   Beyond, in waves of shade and light,
   The hills rolled off into the night.

She saw and heard, but over all
   A sense of some transforming spell,
   The shadow of her sick heart fell.

And still across the wooded space
   The harvest lights of Harden shone,
   And song and jest and laugh went on.

And he, so gentle, true, and strong,
   Of men the bravest and the best,
   Had he, too, scorned her with the rest ?

She strove to drown her sense of wrong,
  And, in her old and simple way,
  To teach her bitter heart to pray.

Poor child ! the prayer, begun in faith,
  Grew to a low, despairing cry
  Of utter misery : " Let me die !

" Oh ! take me from the scornful eyes,
  And hide me where the cruel speech
  And mocking finger may not reach !

" I dare not breathe my mother's name :
  A daughter's right I dare not crave
  To weep above her unblest grave !

" Let me not live until my heart,
  With few to pity, and with none
  To love me, hardens into stone.

" O God ! have mercy on Thy child,
  Whose faith in Thee grows weak and
      small,
  And take me ere I lose it all ! "

A shadow on the moonlight fell,
  And murmuring wind and wave became
  A voice whose burden was her name.

VI. THE BETROTHAL.

Had then God heard her?   Had He
  sent
 His angel down?   In flesh and blood,
 Before her Esek Harden stood!

He laid his hand upon her arm:
 " Dear Mabel, this no more shall be ;
 Who scoffs at you must scoff at me.

" You know rough Esek Harden well ;
 And if he seems no suitor gay,
 And if his hair is touched with gray,

" The maiden grown shall never find
 His heart less warm than when she
  smiled,
 Upon his knees, a little child!"

Her tears of grief were tears of joy,
 As, folded in his strong embrace,
 She looked in Esek Harden's face.

"O truest friend of all!" she said,
 " God bless you for your kindly thought,
 And make me worthy of my lot!"

He led her forth, and, blent in one,
   Beside their happy pathway ran
   The shadows of the maid and man.

He led her through his dewy fields,
   To where the swinging lanterns
     glowed,
   And through the doors the huskers
     showed.

" Good friends and neighbors ! " Esek
     said,
   " I 'm weary of this lonely life ;
   In Mabel see my chosen wife !

" She greets you kindly, one and all ;
   The past is past, and all offence
   Falls harmless from her innocence.

" Henceforth she stands no more
     alone ;
   You know what Esek Harden is ; —
   He brooks no wrong to him or his.

" Now let the merriest tales be told,
   And let the sweetest songs be sung
   That ever made the old heart young !

" For now the lost has found a home ;
   And a lone hearth shall brighter burn,
   As all the household joys return ! "

Oh, pleasantly the harvest-moon,
   Between the shadow of the mows,
   Looked on them through the great elm-
      boughs !

On Mabel's curls of golden hair,
   On Esek's shaggy strength it fell ;
   And the wind whispered, " It is well ! "

THE PROPHECY OF SAMUEL SEWALL.

UP and down the village streets
   Strange are the forms my fancy
     meets,
For the thoughts and things of to-day are
   hid,
And through the veil of a closëd lid
The ancient worthies I see again :
I hear the tap of the elder's cane,

And his awful periwig I see,
And the silver buckles of shoe and knee.
Stately and slow, with thoughtful air,
His black cap hiding his whitened hair,
Walks the Judge of the great Assize,
Samuel Sewall the good and wise.
His face with lines of firmness wrought,
He wears the look of a man unbought,
Who swears to his hurt and changes not;
Yet, touched and softened nevertheless
With the grace of Christian gentleness,
The face that a child would climb to kiss!
True and tender and brave and just,
That man might honor and woman trust.

   Touching and sad, a tale is told,
Like a penitent hymn of the Psalmist old,
Of the fast which the good man lifelong
      kept
With a haunting sorrow that never slept,
As the circling year brought round the
      time
Of an error that left the sting of crime,
When he sat on the bench of the witch-
      craft courts,
With the laws of Moses and Hale's Re-
      ports,

And spake, in the name of both, the word
That gave the witch's neck to the cord,
And piled the oaken planks that pressed
The feeble life from the warlock's breast !
All the day long, from dawn to dawn,
His door was bolted, his curtain drawn ;
No foot on his silent threshold trod,
No eye looked on him save that of God,
As he baffled the ghosts of the dead with
    charms
Of penitent tears, and prayers, and psalms,
And, with precious proofs from the sacred
    word
Of the boundless pity and love of the
    Lord,
His faith confirmed and his trust renewed
That the sin of his ignorance, sorely rued,
Might be washed away in the mingled
    flood
Of his human sorrow and Christ's dear
    blood !

    Green forever the memory be
Of the Judge of the old Theocracy,
Whom even his errors glorified,
Like a far-seen, sunlit mountain-side
By the cloudy shadows which o'er it glide !

Honor and praise to the Puritan
Who the halting step of his age outran,
And, seeing the infinite worth of man
In the priceless gift the Father gave,
In the infinite love that stooped to save,
Dared not brand his brother a slave !
"Who doth such wrong," he was wont to
    say,
In his own quaint, picture-loving way,
"Flings up to Heaven a hand-grenade
Which God shall cast down upon his
    head ! "

Widely as heaven and hell, contrast
That brave old jurist of the past
And the cunning trickster and knave of
    courts
Who the holy features of Truth distorts, —
Ruling as right the will of the strong,
Poverty, crime, and weakness wrong ;
Wide-eared to power, to the wronged and
    weak
Deaf as Egypt's gods of leek ;
Scoffing aside at party's nod
Order of nature and law of God ;
For whose dabbled ermine respect were
    waste,

Reverence folly, and awe misplaced;
Justice of whom 't were vain to seek
As from Koordish robber or Syrian Sheik!
Oh, leave the wretch to his bribes and
      sins;
Let him rot in the web of lies he spins!
To the saintly soul of the early day,
To the Christian judge, let us turn and say:
" Praise and thanks for an honest man! —
Glory to God for the Puritan!"

I see, far southward, this quiet day,
The hills of Newbury rolling away,
With the many tints of the season gay,
Dreamily blending in autumn mist
Crimson, and gold, and amethyst.
Long and low, with dwarf trees crowned,
Plum Island lies, like a whale aground,
A stone's toss over the narrow sound.
Inland, as far as the eye can go,
The hills curve round like a bended bow;
A silver arrow from out them sprung,
I see the shine of the Quasycung;
And, round and round, over valley and
      hill,
Old roads winding, as old roads will,
Here to a ferry, and there to a mill;

And glimpses of chimneys and gabled
    eaves,
Through green elm arches and maple
    leaves, —
Old homesteads sacred to all that can
Gladden or sadden the heart of man,
Over whose thresholds of oak and stone
Life and Death have come and gone !
There pictured tiles in the fireplace
    show,
Great beams sag from the ceiling low,
The dresser glitters with polished wares,
The long clock ticks on the foot-worn
    stairs,
And the low, broad chimney shows the
    crack
By the earthquake made a century back.
Up from their midst springs the village
    spire
With the crest of its cock in the sun
    afire ;
Beyond are orchards and planting lands,
And great salt marshes and glimmering
    sands,
And, where north and south the coast-
    lines run,
The blink of the sea in breeze and sun !

I see it all like a chart unrolled,
But my thoughts are full of the past and
    old,
I hear the tales of my boyhood told ;
And the shadows and shapes of early days
Flit dimly by in the veiling haze,
With measured movement and rhythmic
    chime
Weaving like shuttles my web of rhyme.
I think of the old man wise and good
Who once on yon misty hillsides stood
(A poet who never measured rhyme,
A seer unknown to his dull-eared time),
And, propped on his staff of age, looked
    down,
With his boyhood's love, on his native
    town,
Where, written, as if on its hills and plains,
His burden of prophecy yet remains,
For the voices of wood, and wave, and
    wind
To read in the ear of the musing mind : —

  " As long as Plum Island, to guard the
    coast
As God appointed, shall keep its post ;
As long as a salmon shall haunt the deep
Of Merrimac River, or sturgeon leap ;

As long as pickerel swift and slim,
Or red-backed perch, in Crane Pond
    swim ;
As long as the annual sea-fowl know
Their time to come and their time to go ;
As long as cattle shall roam at will
The green, grass meadows by Turkey
    Hill ;
As long as sheep shall look from the side
Of Oldtown Hill on marishes wide,
And Parker River and salt-sea tide ;
As long as a wandering pigeon shall search
The fields below from his white-oak perch,
When the barley-harvest is ripe and shorn,
And the dry husks fall from the standing
    corn ;
As long as Nature shall not grow old,
Nor drop her work from her doting hold,
And her care for the Indian corn forget,
And the yellow rows in pairs to set ; —
So long shall Christians here be born,
Grow up and ripen as God's sweet
    corn ! —
By the beak of bird, by the breath of frost,
Shall never a holy ear be lost,
But, husked by Death in the Planter's
    sight,
Be sown again in the fields of light ! "

The Island still is purple with plums,
Up the river the salmon comes,
The sturgeon leaps, and the wild-fowl
 feeds
On hillside berries and marish seeds, —
All the beautiful signs remain,
From spring-time sowing to autumn
 rain
The good man's vision returns again !
And let us hope, as well we can,
That the Silent Angel who garners man
May find some grain as of old he found
In the human cornfield ripe and sound,
And the Lord of the Harvest deign to
 own
The precious seed by the fathers sown !

MY PSALM.

MOURN no more my vanished
 years :
 Beneath a tender rain,
 An April rain of smiles and tears,
 My heart is young again.

The west-winds blow, and singing low,
    I hear the glad streams run ;
The windows of my soul I throw
    Wide open to the sun.

No longer forward nor behind
    I look in hope or fear ;
But, grateful, take the good I find,
    The best of now and here.

I plough no more a desert land,
    To harvest weed and tare ;
The manna dropping from God's hand
    Rebukes my painful care.

I break my pilgrim staff, I lay
    Aside the toiling oar ;
The angel sought so far away
    I welcome at my door.

The airs of spring may never play
    Among the ripening corn,
Nor freshness of the flowers of May
    Blow through the autumn morn ;

Yet shall the blue-eyed gentian look
    Through fringëd lids to heaven,

And the pale aster in the brook
  Shall see its image given ;—

The woods shall wear their robes of praise,
  The south-wind softly sigh,
And sweet, calm days in golden haze
  Melt down the amber sky.

Not less shall manly deed and word
  Rebuke an age of wrong ;
The graven flowers that wreathe the
    sword
  Make not the blade less strong.

But smiting hands shall learn to heal, —
  To build as to destroy ;
Nor less my heart for others feel
  That I the more enjoy.

All as God wills, who wisely heeds
  To give or to withhold,
And knoweth more of all my needs
  Than all my prayers have told !

Enough that blessings undeserved
  Have marked my erring track ;
That wheresoe'er my feet have swerved,
  His chastening turned me back ;

That more and more a Providence
    Of love is understood,
Making the springs of time and sense
    Sweet with eternal good ;—

That death seems but a covered way
    Which opens into light,
Wherein no blinded child can stray
    Beyond the Father's sight ;

That care and trial seem at last,
    Through Memory's sunset air,
Like mountain-ranges overpast,
    In purple distance fair;

That all the jarring notes of life
    Seem blending in a psalm,
And all the angles of its strife
    Slow rounding into calm.

And so the shadows fall apart,
    And so the west-winds play;
And all the windows of my heart
    I open to the day.

BARBARA FRIETCHIE.

P from the meadows rich with
    corn,
    Clear in the cool September
    morn,

The clustered spires of Frederick stand
Green-walled by the hills of Maryland.

Round about them orchards sweep,
Apple and peach tree fruited deep,

Fair as the garden of the Lord
To the eyes of the famished rebel horde,

On that pleasant morn of the early fall
When Lee marched over the mountain-
    wall;

Over the mountains winding down,
Horse and foot, into Frederick town.

Forty flags with their silver stars,
Forty flags with their crimson bars,

Flapped in the morning wind : the sun
Of noon looked down, and saw not one.

Up rose old Barbara **Frietchie** then,
Bowed with her fourscore years and ten ;

Bravest of all in Frederick town,
She took up the flag the men hauled down ;

In her attic window the **staff she set,**
To show that one heart was **loyal yet.**

Up the street came **the rebel** tread,
Stonewall Jackson riding ahead.

Under his slouched **hat left and right**
He glanced ; the old flag met his **sight.**

" Halt !" — **the dust-brown ranks stood**
      fast.
" Fire !" — out blazed the rifle-blast.

It shivered the window, pane and sash ;
It rent the banner with seam and gash.

Quick, **as it fell,** from the broken staff
Dame Barbara snatched the silken scarf.

She leaned far out on the window-sill,
And shook it forth with a royal will.

" Shoot, if you must, this old gray head,
But spare your country's flag," she said.

A shade of sadness, a blush of shame,
Over the face of the leader came ;

The nobler nature within him stirred
To life at that woman's deed and word :

" Who touches a hair of yon gray head
Dies like a dog ! March on ! " he said.

All day long through Frederick street
Sounded the tread of marching feet :

All day long that free flag tost
Over the heads of the rebel host.

Ever its torn folds rose and fell
On the loyal winds that loved it well ;

And through the hill-gaps sunset light
Shone over it with a warm good-night.

Barbara Frietchie's work is o'er
And the Rebel rides on his raids no more.

Honor to her ! and let a tear
Fall, for her sake, on Stonewall's bier.

Over Barbara Frietchie's grave,
Flag of Freedom and Union, wave !

Peace and order and beauty draw
Round thy symbol of light and law ;

And ever the stars above look down
On thy stars below in Frederick town !

AMY WENTWORTH.

TO WILLIAM BRADFORD.

A S they who watch by sick-beds find relief
    Unwittingly from the great stress of grief
And anxious care, in fantasies outwrought

From the hearth's embers flickering low,
or caught
From whispering wind, or tread of pass-
ing feet,
Or vagrant memory calling up some sweet
Snatch of old song or romance, whence or
why
They scarcely know or ask, — so, thou
and I,
Nursed in the faith that Truth alone is
strong
In the endurance which outwearies Wrong,
With meek persistence baffling brutal
force,
And trusting God against the universe, —
We, doomed to watch a strife we may not
share
With other weapons than the patriot's
prayer,
Yet owning, with full hearts and moistened
eyes,
The awful beauty of self-sacrifice,
And wrung by keenest sympathy for all
Who give their loved ones for the living
wall
'Twixt law and treason, — in this evil day
May haply find, through automatic play

Of pen and pencil, solace to our pain,
And hearten others with the strength we
    gain.
I know it has been said our times require
No play of art, nor dalliance with the
    lyre,
No weak essay with Fancy's chloroform
To calm the hot, mad pulses of the storm,
But the stern war-blast rather, such as sets
The battle's teeth of serried bayonets,
And pictures grim as Vernet's. Yet with
    these
Some softer tints may blend, and milder
    keys
Relieve the storm-stunned ear. Let us
    keep sweet,
If so we may, our hearts, even while we
    eat
The bitter harvest of our own device
And half a century's moral cowardice.
As Nürnberg sang while Wittenberg defied,
And Kranach painted by his Luther's side,
And through the war-march of the Puritan
The silver stream of Marvell's music ran,
So let the household melodies be sung,
The pleasant pictures on the wall be
    hung, —

So let us hold against the hosts of night
And slavery all our vantage-ground of
    light.
Let Treason boast its savagery, and shake
From its flag-folds its symbol rattlesnake,
Nurse its fine arts, lay human skins in
    tan,
And carve its pipe-bowls from the bones
    of man,
And make the tale of Fijian banquets dull
By drinking whiskey from a loyal skull, —
But let us guard, till this sad war shall
    cease,
(God grant it soon !) the graceful arts of
    peace :
No foes are conquered who the victors
    teach
Their vandal manners and barbaric
    speech.

And while, with hearts of thankfulness, we
    bear
Of the great common burden our full share,
Let none upbraid us that the waves en-
    tice
Thy sea-dipped pencil, or some quaint de-
    vice,

Rhythmic and sweet, beguiles my pen
    away
From the sharp strifes and sorrows of to-
    day.
Thus, while the east - wind keen from
    Labrador
Sings in the leafless elms, and from the
    shore
Of the great sea comes the monotonous
    roar
Of the long-breaking surf, and all the sky
Is gray with cloud, home-bound and dull,
    I try
To time a simple legend to the sounds
Of winds in the woods, and waves on peb-
    bled bounds, —
A song for oars to chime with, such as
    might
Be sung by tired sea - painters, who at
    night
Look from their hemlock camps, by quiet
    cove
Or beach, moon-lighted, on the waves they
    love.
(So hast thou looked, when level sunset
    lay
On the calm bosom of some Eastern bay,

And all the spray-moist rocks and waves
    that rolled
Up the white sand-slopes flashed with
    ruddy gold.)
Something it has — a flavor of the sea,
And the sea's freedom — which reminds
    of thee.
Its faded picture, dimly smiling down
From the blurred fresco of the ancient
    town,
I have not touched with warmer tints in
    vain,
If, in this dark, sad year, it steals one
    thought from pain.

Her fingers shame the ivory keys
    They dance so light along ;
The bloom upon her parted lips
    Is sweeter than the song.

O perfumed suitor, spare thy smiles !
    Her thoughts are not of thee ;
She better loves the salted wind,
    The voices of the sea.

Her heart is like an outbound ship
  That at its anchor swings ;
The murmur of the stranded shell
  Is in the song she sings.

She sings, and, smiling, hears her praise,
  But dreams the while of one
Who watches from his sea-blown deck
  The icebergs in the sun.

She questions all the winds that blow,
  And every fog-wreath dim,
And bids the sea-birds flying north
  Bear messages to him.

She speeds them with the thanks of men
  He perilled life to save,
And grateful prayers like holy oil
  To smooth for him the wave.

Brown Viking of the fishing-smack !
  Fair toast of all the town ! —
The skipper's jerkin ill beseems
  The lady's silken gown !

But ne'er shall Amy Wentworth wear
  For him the blush of shame

Who dares to set his manly gifts
    Against her ancient name.

The stream is brightest at its spring,
    And blood is not like wine ;
Nor honored less than he who heirs
    Is he who founds a line.

Full lightly shall the prize be won,
    If love be Fortune's spur ;
And never maiden stoops to him
    Who lifts himself to her.

Her home is brave in Jaffrey Street,
    With stately stairways worn
By feet of old Colonial knights
    And ladies gentle-born.

Still green about its ample porch
    The English ivy twines,
Trained back to show in English oak
    The herald's carven signs.

And on her, from the wainscot old,
    Ancestral faces frown, —
And this has worn the soldier's sword,
    And that the judge's gown.

But, strong of will and proud as they,
 She walks the gallery floor
As if she trod her sailor's deck
 By stormy Labrador !

The sweetbrier blooms on Kittery-side,
 And green are Elliot's bowers ;
Her garden is the pebbled beach,
 The mosses are her flowers.

She looks across the harbor-bar
 To see the white gulls fly ;
His greeting from the Northern sea
 Is in their clanging cry.

She hums a song, and dreams that he,
 As in its romance old,
Shall homeward ride with silken sails
And masts of beaten gold !

Oh, rank is good, and gold is fair,
 And high and low mate ill ;
But love has never known a law
 Beyond its own sweet will !

SNOW-BOUND.

A WINTER IDYL.

———

TO THE MEMORY

OF

THE HOUSEHOLD IT DESCRIBES,

THIS POEM IS DEDICATED BY THE AUTHOR.

———

"As the Spirits of Darkness be stronger in the dark, so
Good Spirits, which be Angels of Light, are augmented not
only by the Divine Light of the Sun, but also by our common Wood Fire: and as the Celestial Fire drives away dark
spirits, so also this our Fire of Wood doth the same." — COR.
AGRIPPA, *Occult Philosophy*, Book I. ch. v.

"Announced by all the trumpets of the sky,
    Arrives the snow, and, driving o'er the fields,
    Seems nowhere to alight: the whited air
    Hides hills and woods, the river and the heaven,
    And veils the farm-house at the garden's end.
    The sled and traveller stopped, the courier's feet
    Delayed, all friends shut out, the housemates sit
    Around the radiant fireplace, enclosed
    In a tumultuous privacy of storm."
                    EMERSON. *The Snow-Storm.*

THE sun that brief December day
    Rose cheerless over hills of gray,
    And, darkly circled, gave at noon
A sadder light than waning moon.

Slow tracing down the thickening sky
Its mute and ominous prophecy,
A portent seeming less than threat,
It sank from sight before it set.
A chill no coat, however stout,
Of homespun stuff could quite shut out,
A hard, dull bitterness of cold,
That checked, mid-vein, the circling race
Of life-blood in the sharpened face,
The coming of the snow-storm told.
The wind blew east; we heard the roar
Of Ocean on his wintry shore,
And felt the strong pulse throbbing there
Beat with low rhythm our inland air.

Meanwhile we did our nightly chores, —
Brought in the wood from out of doors,
Littered the stalls, and from the mows
Raked down the herd's-grass for the cows :
Heard the horse whinnying for his corn ;
And, sharply clashing horn on horn,
Impatient down the stanchion rows
The cattle shake their walnut bows ;
While, peering from his early perch
Upon the scaffold's pole of birch,
The cock his crested helmet bent
And down his querulous challenge sent.

Unwarmed by any sunset light
The gray day darkened into night,
A night made hoary with the swarm,
And whirl-dance of the blinding storm,
As zigzag, wavering to and fro,
Crossed and recrossed the wingëd snow :
And ere the early bedtime came
The white drift piled the window-frame,
And through the glass the clothes - line
　　　posts
Looked in like tall and sheeted ghosts.

So all night long the storm roared on :
The morning broke without a sun ;
In tiny spherule traced with lines
Of Nature's geometric signs,
In starry flake, and pellicle,
All day the hoary meteor fell ;
And, when the second morning shone,
We looked upon a world unknown,
On nothing we could call our own.
Around the glistening wonder bent
The blue walls of the firmament,
No cloud above, no earth below, —
A universe of sky and snow !
The old familiar sights of ours
Took marvellous shapes ; strange domes
　　　and towers

Rose up where sty or corn-crib stood,
Or garden-wall, or belt of wood ;
A smooth white mound the brush - pile
    showed,
A fenceless drift what once was road ;
The bridle-post an old man sat
With loose - flung coat and high cocked
    hat ;
The well-curb had a Chinese roof ;
And even the long sweep, high aloof,
In its slant splendor, seemed to tell
Of Pisa's leaning miracle.

A prompt, decisive man, no breath
Our father wasted : " Boys, a path ! "
Well pleased (for when did farmer boy
Count such a summons less than joy ?)
Our buskins on our feet we drew ;
With mittened hands, and caps drawn low,
To guard our necks and ears from snow,
We cut the solid whiteness through.
And where the drift was deepest, made
A tunnel walled and overlaid
With dazzling crystal : we had read
Of rare Aladdin's wondrous cave,
And to our own his name we gave,
With many a wish the luck were ours

To test his lamp's supernal powers.
We reached the barn with merry din,
And roused the prisoned brutes within.
The old horse thrust his long head out,
And grave with wonder gazed about;
The cock his lusty greeting said,
And forth his speckled harem led ;
The oxen lashed their tails, and hooked,
And mild reproach of hunger looked ;
The hornëd patriarch of the sheep,
Like Egypt's Amun roused from sleep,
Shook his sage head with gesture mute,
And emphasized with stamp of foot.

All day the gusty north-wind bore
The loosening drift its breath before ;
Low circling round its southern zone,
The sun through dazzling snow-mist shone.
No church-bell lent its Christian tone
To the savage air, no social smoke
Curled over woods of snow-hung oak.
A solitude made more intense
By dreary-voicëd elements,
The shrieking of the mindless wind,
The moaning tree-boughs swaying blind,
And on the glass the unmeaning beat
Of ghostly finger-tips of sleet.

Beyond the circle of our hearth
No welcome sound of toil or mirth
Unbound the spell, and testified
Of human life and thought outside.
We minded that the sharpest ear
The buried brooklet could not hear,
The music of whose liquid lip
Had been to us companionship,
And, in our lonely life, had grown
To have an almost human tone.

As night drew on, and, from the crest
Of wooded knolls that ridged the west,
The sun, a snow-blown traveller, sank
From sight beneath the smothering bank,
We piled, with care, our nightly stack
Of wood against the chimney-back, —
The oaken log, green, huge, and thick,
And on its top the stout back-stick ;
The knotty forestick laid apart,
And filled between with curious art
The ragged brush ; then, hovering near,
We watched the first red blaze appear,
Heard the sharp crackle, caught the gleam
On whitewashed wall and sagging beam,
Until the old, rude-furnished room
Burst, flower-like, into rosy bloom ;

While radiant with a mimic flame
Outside the sparkling drift became,
And through the bare-boughed lilac-tree
Our own warm hearth seemed blazing free.
The crane and pendent trammels showed,
The Turks' heads on the andirons glowed ;
While childish fancy, prompt to tell
The meaning of the miracle,
Whispered the old rhyme : " *Under the tree,*
When fire outdoors burns merrily,
There the witches are making tea."

The moon above the eastern wood
Shone at its full ; the hill-range stood
Transfigured in the silver flood,
Its blown snows flashing cold and keen,
Dead white, save where some sharp ravine
Took shadow, or the sombre green
Of hemlocks turned to pitchy black
Against the whiteness at their back.
For such a world and such a night
Most fitting that unwarming light,
Which only seemed where'er it fell
To make the coldness visible.

Shut in from all the world without,
We sat the clean-winged hearth about,

Content to let the north-wind roar
In baffled rage at pane and door,
While the red logs before us beat
The frost-line back with tropic heat ;
And ever, when a louder blast
Shook beam and rafter as it passed,
The merrier up its roaring draught
The great throat of the chimney laughed ;
The house-dog on his paws outspread
Laid to the fire his drowsy head,
The cat's dark silhouette on the wall
A couchant tiger's seemed to fall ;
And, for the winter fireside meet,
Between the andirons' straddling feet,
The mug of cider simmered slow,
The apples sputtered in a row,
And, close at hand, the basket stood
With nuts from brown October's wood.

What matter how the night behaved ?
What matter how the north-wind raved ?
Blow high, blow low, not all its snow
Could quench our hearth-fire's ruddy glow.
O Time and Change ! — with hair as gray
As was my sire's that winter day,
How strange it seems, with so much gone
Of life and love, to still live on !

Ah, brother! only I and thou
Are left of all that circle now, —
The dear home faces whereupon
That fitful firelight paled and shone.
Henceforward, listen as we will,
The voices of that hearth are still;
Look where we may, the wide earth o'er
Those lighted faces smile no more.
We tread the paths their feet have worn,
    We sit beneath their orchard trees,
    We hear, like them, the hum of bees
And rustle of the bladed corn;
We turn the pages that they read,
    Their written words we linger o'er,
But in the sun they cast no shade,
No voice is heard, no sign is made,
    No step is on the conscious floor!
Yet Love will dream, and Faith will trust,
(Since He who knows our need is just),
That somehow, somewhere, meet we must.
Alas for him who never sees
The stars shine through his cypress-trees!
Who, hopeless, lays his dead away,
Nor looks to see the breaking day
Across the mournful marbles play!
Who hath not learned, in hours of faith,
    The truth to flesh and sense unknown,

That Life is ever lord of Death,
  And Love can never lose its own !

We sped the time with stories old,
Wrought puzzles out, and riddles told,
Or stammered from our school-book lore
" The Chief of Gambia's golden shore."
How often since, when all the land
Was clay in Slavery's shaping hand,
As if a far-blown trumpet stirred
The languorous sin-sick air, I heard :
" *Does not the voice of reason cry*,
  Claim the first right which Nature gave,
From the red scourge of bondage fly,
  Nor deign to live a burdened slave !"
Our father rode again his ride
On Memphremagog's wooded side ;
Sat down again to moose and samp
In trapper's hut and Indian camp ;
Lived o'er the old idyllic ease
Beneath St. François' hemlock-trees ;
Again for him the moonlight shone
On Norman cap and bodiced zone ;
Again he heard the violin play
Which led the village dance away,
And mingled in its merry whirl
The grandam and the laughing girl.

Or, nearer home, our steps he led
Where Salisbury's level marshes spread
    Mile-wide as flies the laden bee ;
Where merry mowers, hale and strong,
Swept, scythe on scythe, their swaths along
    The low green prairies of the sea.
We shared the fishing off Boar's Head,
    And round the rocky Isles of Shoals
    The hake-broil on the drift-wood coals ;
The chowder on the sand-beach made,
Dipped by the hungry, steaming hot,
With spoons of clam-shell from the pot.
We heard the tales of witchcraft old,
And dream and sign and marvel told
To sleepy listeners as they lay
Stretched idly on the salted hay,
Adrift along the winding shores,
    When favoring breezes deigned to blow
    The square sail of the gundelow
And idle lay the useless oars.

Our mother, while she turned her wheel
Or run the new-knit stocking-heel,
Told how the Indian hordes came down
At midnight on Cocheco town,
And how her own great-uncle bore
His cruel scalp-mark to fourscore.

Recalling, in her fitting phrase,
So rich and picturesque and free,
(The common unrhymed poetry
Of simple life and country ways),
The story of her early days, —
She made us welcome to her home;
Old hearths grew wide to give us room;
We stole with her a frightened look
At the gray wizard's conjuring-book,
The fame whereof went far and wide
Through all the simple country side;
We heard the hawks at twilight play,
The boat-horn on Piscataqua,
The loon's weird laughter far away;
We fished her little trout-brook, knew
What flowers in wood and meadow grew,
What sunny hillsides autumn-brown
She climbed to shake the ripe nuts down,
Saw where in sheltered cove and bay
The ducks' black squadron anchored lay,
And heard the wild-geese calling loud
Beneath the gray November cloud.

Then, haply, with a look more grave,
And soberer tone, some tale she gave
From painful Sewell's ancient tome,
Beloved in every Quaker home,

Of faith fire-winged by martyrdom,
Or Chalkley's Journal, old and quaint, —
Gentlest of skippers, rare sea-saint ! —
Who when the dreary calms prevailed,
And water-butt and bread-cask failed,
And cruel, hungry eyes pursued
His portly presence mad for food,
With dark hints muttered under breath
Of casting lots for life or death,
Offered, if Heaven withheld supplies,
To be himself the sacrifice.
Then, suddenly, as if to save
The good man from his living grave,
A ripple on the water grew,
A school of porpoise flashed in view.
" Take, eat," he said, " and be content;
These fishes in my stead are sent
By Him who gave the tangled ram
To spare the child of Abraham."

Our uncle, innocent of books,
Was rich in lore of fields and brooks,
The ancient teachers never dumb
Of Nature's unhoused lyceum.
In moons and tides and weather wise,
He read the clouds as prophecies,
And foul or fair could well divine,

By many an occult hint and sign,
Holding the cunning-warded keys
To all the woodcraft mysteries;
Himself to Nature's heart so near
That all her voices in his ear
Of beast or bird had meanings clear,
Like Apollonius of old,
Who knew the tales the sparrows told,
Or Hermes who interpreted
What the sage cranes of Nilus said:
Content to live where life began;
A simple, guileless, childlike man,
Strong only on his native grounds,
The little world of sights and sounds
Whose girdle was the parish bounds,
Whereof his fondly partial pride
The common features magnified,
As Surrey hills to mountains grew
In White of Selborne's loving view, —
He told how teal and loon he shot,
And how the eagle's eggs he got,
The feats on pond and river done,
The prodigies of rod and gun;
Till, warming with the tales he told,
Forgotten was the outside cold,
The bitter wind unheeded blew,
From ripening corn the pigeons flew,

The partridge drummed i' the wood, the
    mink
Went fishing down the river-brink.
In fields with bean or clover gay,
The woodchuck, like a hermit gray,
    Peered from the doorway of his cell;
The muskrat plied the mason's trade,
And tier by tier his mud-walls laid;
And from the shagbark overhead
    The grizzled squirrel dropped his shell.

Next, the dear aunt, whose smile of cheer
And voice in dreams I see and hear, —
The sweetest woman ever Fate
Perverse denied a household mate,
Who, lonely, homeless, not the less
Found peace in love's unselfishness,
And welcome wheresoe'er she went,
A calm and gracious element,
Whose presence seemed the sweet income
And womanly atmosphere of home, —
Called up her girlhood memories,
The huskings and the apple-bees,
The sleigh-rides and the summer sails,
Weaving through all the poor details
And homespun warp of circumstance
A golden woof-thread of romance.

For well she kept her genial mood
And simple faith of maidenhood ;
Before her still a cloud-land lay,
The mirage loomed across her way ;
The morning dew, that dries so soon
With others, glistened at her noon ;
Through years of toil and soil and care,
From glossy tress to thin gray hair,
All unprofaned she held apart
The virgin fancies of the heart.
Be shame to him of woman born
Who hath for such but thought of scorn.

There, too, our elder sister plied
Her evening task the stand beside ;
A full, rich nature, free to trust,
Truthful and almost sternly just,
Impulsive, earnest, prompt to act,
And make her generous thought a fact,
Keeping with many a light disguise
The secret of self-sacrifice.
O heart sore-tried ! thou hast the best
That Heaven itself could give thee, — rest,
Rest from all bitter thoughts and things !
How many a poor one's blessing went
With thee beneath the low green tent
Whose curtain never outward swings !

As one who held herself a part
Of all she saw, and let her heart
  Against the household bosom lean,
Upon the motley-braided mat
Our youngest and our dearest sat,
Lifting her large, sweet, asking eyes,
  Now bathed in the unfading green
And holy peace of Paradise.
Oh, looking from some heavenly hill,
  Or from the shade of saintly palms,
  Or silver reach of river calms,
Do those large eyes behold me still ?
With me one little year ago : —
The chill weight of the winter snow
  For months upon her grave has lain ;
And now, when summer south-winds blow
  And brier and harebell bloom again,
I tread the pleasant paths we trod,
I see the violet-sprinkled sod
Whereon she leaned, too frail and weak
The hillside flowers she loved to seek,
Yet following me where'er I went
With dark eyes full of love's content.
The birds are glad ; the brier-rose fills
The air with sweetness ; all the hills
Stretch green to June's unclouded sky ;
But still I wait with ear and eye

For something gone which should be nigh,
A loss in all familiar things,
In flower that blooms, and bird that sings.
And yet, dear heart ! remembering thee,
　Am I not richer than of old ?
Safe in thy immortality,
　What change can reach the wealth I
　　hold ?
　What chance can mar the pearl and
　　gold
Thy love hath left in trust with me ?
And while in life's late afternoon,
　Where cool and long the shadows grow,
I walk to meet the night that soon
　Shall shape and shadow overflow,
I cannot feel that thou art far,
Since near at need the angels are ;
And when the sunset gates unbar,
　Shall I not see thee waiting stand,
And, white against the evening star,
　The welcome of thy beckoning hand ?

Brisk wielder of the birch and rule,
The master of the district school
Held at the fire his favored place,
Its warm glow lit a laughing face
Fresh - hued and fair, where scarce ap-
　　peared

The uncertain prophecy of beard.
He teased the mitten-blinded cat,
Played cross-pins on my uncle's hat,
Sang songs, and told us what befalls
In classic Dartmouth's college halls.
Born the wild Northern hills among,
From whence his yeoman father wrung
By patient toil subsistence scant,
Not competence and yet not want,
He early gained the power to pay
His cheerful, self-reliant way;
Could doff at ease his scholar's gown
To peddle wares from town to town;
Or through the long vacation's reach
In lonely lowland districts teach,
Where all the droll experience found
At stranger hearths in boarding round,
The moonlit skater's keen delight,
The sleigh-drive through the frosty night,
The rustic party, with its rough
Accompaniment of blind-man's-buff,
And whirling plate, and forfeits paid,
His winter task a pastime made.
Happy the snow-locked homes wherein
He tuned his merry violin,
Or played the athlete in the barn,
Or held the good dame's winding-yarn,

Or mirth-provoking versions told
Of classic legends rare and old,
Wherein the scenes of Greece and Rome
Had all the commonplace of home,
And little seemed at best the odds
'Twixt Yankee pedlers and old gods;
Where Pindus-born Arachthus took
The guise of any grist-mill brook,
And dread Olympus at his will
Became a huckleberry hill.

A careless boy that night he seemed;
  But at his desk he had the look
And air of one who wisely schemed,
  And hostage from the future took
  In trainéd thought and lore of book.
Large-brained, clear-eyed, of such as he
Shall Freedom's young apostles be,
Who, following in War's bloody trail,
Shall every lingering wrong assail;
All chains from limb and spirit strike,
Uplift the black and white alike;
Scatter before their swift advance
The darkness and the ignorance,
The pride, the lust, the squalid sloth,
Which nurtured Treason's monstrous
      growth,

Made murder pastime, and the hell
Of prison-torture possible;
The cruel lie of caste refute,
Old forms remould, and substitute
For Slavery's lash the freeman's will,
For blind routine, wise-handed skill;
A school-house plant on every hill,
Stretching in radiate nerve-lines thence
The quick wires of intelligence;
Till North and South together brought
Shall own the same electric thought,
In peace a common flag salute,
And, side by side in labor's free
And unresentful rivalry,
Harvest the fields wherein they fought.

Another guest that winter night
Flashed back from lustrous eyes the light.
Unmarked by time, and yet not young,
The honeyed music of her tongue
And words of meekness scarcely told
A nature passionate and bold,
Strong, self-concentred, spurning guide,
Its milder features dwarfed beside
Her unbent will's majestic pride.
She sat among us, at the best,
A not unfeared, half-welcome guest,
Rebuking with her cultured phrase

Our homeliness of words and ways.
A certain pard-like, treacherous grace
   Swayed the lithe limbs and dropped the
      lash,
   Lent the white teeth their dazzling flash ;
   And under low brows, black with night,
   Rayed out at times a dangerous light ;
The sharp heat-lightnings of her face
Presaging ill to him whom Fate
Condemned to share her love or hate.
A woman tropical, intense
In thought and act, in soul and sense,
She blended in a like degree
The vixen and the devotee,
Revealing with each freak or feint
   The temper of Petruchio's Kate,
The raptures of Siena's saint.
Her tapering hand and rounded wrist
Had facile power to form a fist ;
The warm, dark languish of her eyes
Was never safe from wrath's surprise.
Brows saintly calm and lips devout
Knew every change of scowl and pout ;
And the sweet voice had notes more high
And shrill for social battle-cry.

Since then what old cathedral town
Has missed her pilgrim staff and gown,

What convent-gate has held its lock
Against the challenge of her knock!
Through Smyrna's plague-hushed thor-
        oughfares,
Up sea-set Malta's rocky stairs,
Gray olive slopes of hills that hem
Thy tombs and shrines, Jerusalem,
Or startling on her desert throne
The crazy Queen of Lebanon
With claims fantastic as her own,
Her tireless feet have held their way;
And still, unrestful, bowed, and gray,
She watches under Eastern skies,
    With hope each day renewed and fresh,
    The Lord's quick coming in the flesh,
Whereof she dreams and prophesies!

Where'er her troubled path may be,
    The Lord's sweet pity with her go!
The outward wayward life we see,
    The hidden springs we may not know.
Nor is it given us to discern
    What threads the fatal sisters spun,
    Through what ancestral years has run
The sorrow with the woman born,
What forged her cruel chain of moods,
What set her feet in solitudes,

And held the love within her mute,
What mingled madness in the blood,
  A life-long discord and annoy,
  Water of tears with oil of joy,
And hid within the folded bud
  Perversities of flower and fruit.
It is not ours to separate
The tangled skein of will and fate,
To show what metes and bounds should
      stand
Upon the soul's debatable land,
And between choice and Providence
Divide the circle of events;
But He who knows our frame is just,
Merciful and compassionate,
And full of sweet assurances
And hope for all the language is,
That He remembereth we are dust!

At last the great logs, crumbling low,
Sent out a dull and duller glow,
The bull's-eye watch that hung in view,
Ticking its weary circuit through,
Pointed with mutely warning sign
Its black hand to the hour of nine.
That sign the pleasant circle broke:
My uncle ceased his pipe to smoke,

Knocked from its bowl the refuse gray,
And laid it tenderly away,
Then roused himself to safely cover
The dull red brands with ashes over.
And while, with care, our mother laid
The work aside, her steps she stayed
One moment, seeking to express
Her grateful sense of happiness
For food and shelter, warmth and health,
And love's contentment more than wealth,
With simple wishes (not the weak,
Vain prayers which no fulfilment seek,
But such as warm the generous heart,
O'er-prompt to do with Heaven its part)
That none might lack, that bitter night,
For bread and clothing, warmth and light.

Within our beds awhile we heard
The wind that round the gables roared,
With now and then a ruder shock,
Which made our very bedsteads rock.
We heard the loosened clapboards tost,
The board-nails snapping in the frost ;
And on us, through the unplastered wall,
Felt the light sifted snow-flakes fall.
But sleep stole on, as sleep will do
When hearts are light and life is new ;
Faint and more faint the murmurs grew,

Till in the summer-land of dreams
They softened to the sound of streams,
Low stir of leaves, and dip of oars,
And lapsing waves on quiet shores.

Next morn we wakened with the shout
Of merry voices high and clear ;
And saw the teamsters drawing near
To break the drifted highways out.
Down the long hillside treading slow
We saw the half-buried oxen go,
Shaking the snow from heads uptost,
Their straining nostrils white with frost.
Before our door the straggling train
Drew up, an added team to gain.
The elders threshed their hands a-cold,
   Passed, with the cider-mug, their jokes
   From lip to lip ; the younger folks
Down the loose snow-banks, wrestling,
      rolled,
Then toiled again the cavalcade
   O'er windy hill, through clogged ra-
      vine,
   And woodland paths that wound be-
      tween
Low drooping pine-boughs winter-weighed.
From every barn a team afoot,
At every house a new recruit,

Where, drawn by Nature's subtlest law
Haply the watchful young men saw
Sweet doorway pictures of the curls
And curious eyes of merry girls,
Lifting their hands in mock defence
Against the snow-ball's compliments,
And reading in each missive tost
The charm with Eden never lost.

We heard once more the sleigh-bells'
    sound;
    And, following where the teamsters led,
The wise old Doctor went his round,
Just pausing at our door to say,
In the brief autocratic way
Of one who, prompt at Duty's call,
Was free to urge her claim on all,
    That some poor neighbor sick abed
At night our mother's aid would need.
For, one in generous thought and deed,
    What mattered in the sufferer's sight
    The Quaker matron's inward light,
The Doctor's mail of Calvin's creed?
All hearts confess the saints elect
    Who, twain in faith, in love agree,
And melt not in an acid sect
    The Christian pearl of charity!

So days went on : a week had passed
Since the great world was heard from last.
The Almanac we studied o'er,
Read and reread our little store,
Of books and pamphlets, scarce a score ;
One harmless novel, mostly hid
From younger eyes, a book forbid,
And poetry, (or good or bad,
A single book was all we had,)
Where Ellwood's meek, drab-skirted Muse,
    A stranger to the heathen Nine,
    Sang, with a somewhat nasal whine,
The wars of David and the Jews.
At last the floundering carrier bore
The village paper to our door.
Lo ! broadening outward as we read,
To warmer zones the horizon spread ;
In panoramic length unrolled
We saw the marvels that it told.
Before us passed the painted Creeks,
    And daft McGregor on his raids
    In Costa Rica's everglades.
And up Taygetos winding slow
Rode Ypsilanti's Mainote Greeks,
A Turk's head at each saddle-bow !
Welcome to us its week-old news,
Its corner for the rustic Muse,

Its monthly gauge of snow and rain,
Its record, mingling in a breath
The wedding knell and dirge of death ;
Jest, anecdote, and love-lorn tale,
The latest culprit sent to jail ;
Its hue and cry of stolen and lost,
Its vendue sales and goods at cost,
  And traffic calling loud for gain.
We felt the stir of hall and street,
The pulse of life that round us beat ;
The chill embargo of the snow
Was melted in the genial glow ;
Wide swung again our ice-locked door,
And all the world was ours once more !

Clasp, Angel of the backward look
  And folded wings of ashen gray
  And voice of echoes far away,
The brazen covers of thy book ;
The weird palimpsest old and vast,
Wherein thou hid'st the spectral past ;
Where, closely mingling, pale and glow
The characters of joy and woe ;
The monographs of outlived years,
Or smile-illumed or dim with tears,
  Green hills of life that slope to death,
And haunts of home, whose vistaed trees

Shade off to mournful cypresses
  With the white amaranths underneath.
Even while I look, I can but heed
  The restless sands' incessant fall,
Importunate hours that hours succeed,
Each clamorous with its own sharp need,
  And duty keeping pace with all.
Shut down and clasp the heavy lids ;
I hear again the voice that bids
The dreamer leave his dream midway
For larger hopes and graver fears :
Life greatens in these later years,
The century's aloe flowers to-day !
Yet haply, in some lull of life,
Some Truce of God which breaks its
      strife,
The worldling's eyes shall gather dew,
  Dreaming in throngful city ways
Of winter joys his boyhood knew ;
And dear and early friends — the few
Who yet remain — shall pause to view
  These Flemish pictures of old days ;
Sit with me by the homestead hearth,
And stretch the hands of memory forth
  To warm them at the wood-fire's blaze !
And thanks untraced to lips unknown
Shall greet me like the odors blown

From unseen meadows newly mown,
Or lilies floating in some pond,
Wood-fringed, the wayside gaze beyond ;
The traveller owns the grateful sense
Of sweetness near, he knows not whence,
And, pausing, takes with forehead bare
The benediction of the air.

THE WRECK OF RIVERMOUTH.

IVERMOUTH Rocks are fair to
        see,
    By dawn or sunset shone across,
When the ebb of the sea has left them free,
    To dry their fringes of gold-green moss :
For there the river comes winding down,
From salt sea - meadows and uplands
        brown,
And waves on the outer rocks afoam
Shout to its waters, " Welcome home ! "

And fair are the sunny isles in view
    East of the grisly Head of the Boar,

And Agamenticus lifts its blue
  Disk of a cloud the woodlands o'er ;
And southerly, when the tide is down,
'Twixt white sea-waves and sand-hills
    brown,
The beach-birds dance and the gray gulls
    wheel
Over a floor of burnished steel.

Once, in the old Colonial days,
  Two hundred years ago and more,
A boat sailed down through the winding
    ways
  Of Hampton River to that low shore,
Full of a goodly company
Sailing out on the summer sea,
Veering to catch the land-breeze light,
With the Boar to left and the Rocks to
    right.

In Hampton meadows, where mowers
    laid
  Their scythes to the swaths of salted
    grass,
" Ah, well-a-day ! our hay must be made ! "
  A young man sighed, who saw them
    pass.

Loud laughed his fellows to see him stand
Whetting his scythe with a listless hand,
Hearing a voice in a far-off song,
Watching a white hand beckoning long.

" Fie on the witch ! " cried a merry girl,
　As they rounded the point where Goody
　　Cole
Sat by her door with her wheel atwirl,
　A bent and blear-eyed poor old soul.
" Oho ! " she muttered, " ye 're brave to-
　　day !
But I hear the little waves laugh and say,
' The broth will be cold that waits at home ;
For it 's one to go, but another to come ! ' "

" She 's cursed," said the skipper ; " speak
　　her fair :
　I 'm scary always to see her shake
Her wicked head, with its wild gray hair,
　And nose like a hawk, and eyes like a
　　snake."
But merrily still, with laugh and shout,
From Hampton River the boat sailed out,
Till the huts and the flakes on Star seemed
　　nigh,
And they lost the scent of the pines of
　　Rye.

They dropped their lines in the lazy tide,
  Drawing up haddock and mottled cod ;
They saw not the Shadow that walked
      beside,
    They heard not the feet with silence
      shod.
But thicker and thicker a hot mist grew,
Shot by the lightnings through and
      through ;
And muffled growls, like the growl of a
      beast,
Ran along the sky from west to east.

Then the skipper looked from the darken-
      ing sea
  Up to the dimmed and wading sun ;
But he spake like a brave man cheerily,
    "Yet there is time for our homeward
      run."
Veering and tacking, they backward wore ;
And just as a breath from the woods
      ashore
Blew out to whisper of danger past,
The wrath of the storm came down at
      last !

The skipper hauled at the heavy sail :
  "God be our help !" he only cried,

As the roaring gale, like the stroke of a
   flail,
  Smote the boat on its starboard side.
The Shoalsmen looked, but saw alone
Dark films of rain-cloud slantwise blown,
Wild rocks lit up by the lightning's glare,
The strife and torment of sea and air.

Goody Cole looked out from her door :
  The Isles of Shoals were drowned and
    gone,
Scarcely she saw the Head of the Boar
  Toss the foam from tusks of stone.
She clasped her hands with a grip of pain,
The tear on her cheek was not of rain :
" They are lost," she muttered, " boat and
   crew !
Lord, forgive me ! my words were true ! "

Suddenly seaward swept the squall ;
  The low sun smote through cloudy
   rack ;
The Shoals stood clear in the light, and
   all
  The trend of the coast lay hard and
   black.
But far and wide as eye could reach,
No life was seen upon wave or beach ;

The boat that went out at morning never
Sailed back again into Hampton River.

O mower, lean on thy bended snath,
    Look from the meadows green and low:
The wind of the sea is a waft of death,
    The waves are singing a song of woe!
By silent river, by moaning sea,
Long and vain shall thy watching be:
Never again shall the sweet voice call,
Never the white hand rise and fall!

O Rivermouth Rocks, how sad a sight
    Ye saw in the light of breaking day!
Dead faces looking up cold and white
    From sand and seaweed where they lay.
The mad old witch-wife wailed and wept,
And cursed the tide as it backward crept:
"Crawl back, crawl back, blue water-snake!
Leave your dead for the hearts that
        break!"

Solemn it was in that old day
    In Hampton town and its log-built
        church,
Where side by side the coffins lay
    And the mourners stood in aisle and
        porch.

In the singing-seats young eyes were dim,
The voices faltered that raised the hymn,
And Father Dalton, grave and stern,
Sobbed through his prayer and wept in
    turn.

But his ancient colleague did not pray;
  Under the weight of his fourscore years
He stood apart with the iron-gray
  Of his strong brows knitted to hide his
    tears;
And a fair-faced woman of doubtful fame,
Linking her own with his honored name,
Subtle as sin, at his side withstood
The felt reproach of her neighborhood.

Apart with them, like them forbid,
  Old Goody Cole looked drearily round,
As, two by two, with their faces hid,
  The mourners walked to the burying-
    ground.
She let the staff from her clasped hands
    fall:
"Lord, forgive us! we're sinners all!"
And the voice of the old man answered
    her:
"Amen!" said Father Bachiler.

So, as I sat upon Appledore
In the calm of a closing summer day,
And the broken lines of Hampton shore
In purple mist of cloudland lay,
The Rivermouth Rocks their story told;
And waves aglow with sunset gold,
Rising and breaking in steady chime,
Beat the rhythm and kept the time.

And the sunset paled, and warmed once
    more
With a softer, tenderer after-glow;
In the east was moon-rise, with boats off-
    shore
And sails in the distance drifting slow.
The beacon glimmered from Portsmouth
    bar,
The White Isle kindled its great red star;
And life and death in my old-time lay
Mingled in peace like the night and day!

THE DEAD SHIP OF HARPSWELL.

WHAT flecks the outer gray beyond
  The sundown's golden trail?
The white flash of a sea-bird's wing,
  Or gleam of slanting sail?
Let young eyes watch from Neck and
    Point,
  And sea-worn elders pray, —
The ghost of what was once a ship
  Is sailing up the bay!

From gray sea-fog, from icy drift,
  From peril and from pain,
The home-bound fisher greets thy lights,
  O hundred-harbored Maine!
But many a keel shall seaward turn,
  And many a sail outstand,
When, tall and white, the Dead Ship
    looms
  Against the dusk of land.

She rounds the headland's bristling pines;
  She threads the isle-set bay;

No spur of breeze can speed her on,
   Nor ebb of tide delay.
Old men still walk the Isle of Orr
   Who tell her date and name,
Old shipwrights sit in Freeport yards
   Who hewed her oaken frame.

What weary doom of baffled quest,
   Thou sad sea-ghost, is thine?
What makes thee in the haunts of home
   A wonder and a sign?
No foot is on thy silent deck,
   Upon thy helm no hand;
No ripple hath the soundless wind
   That smites thee from the land!

For never comes the ship to port,
   Howe'er the breeze may be;
Just when she nears the waiting shore
   She drifts again to sea.
No tack of sail, nor turn of helm,
   Nor sheer of veering side;
Stern-fore she drives to sea and night,
   Against the wind and tide.

In vain o'er Harpswell Neck the star
   Of evening guides her in;

In vain for her the lamps are lit
　Within thy tower, Seguin !
In vain the harbor-boat shall hail,
　In vain the pilot call ;
No hand shall reef her spectral sail,
　Or let her anchor fall.

Shake, brown old wives, with dreary joy,
　Your gray-head hints of ill ;
And, over sick-beds whispering low,
　Your prophecies fulfil.
Some home amid yon birchen trees
　Shall drape its door with woe ;
And slowly where the Dead Ship sails,
　The burial boat shall row !

From Wolf Neck and from Flying Point,
　From island and from main,
From sheltered cove and tided creek,
　Shall glide the funeral train.
The dead-boat with the bearers four,
　The mourners at her stern, —
And one shall go the silent way
　Who shall no more return !

And men shall sigh, and women weep,
　Whose dear ones pale and pine,

And sadly over sunset seas
   Await the ghostly sign.
They know not that its sails are filled
   By pity's tender breath,
Nor see the Angel at the helm
   Who steers the Ship of Death !

ABRAHAM DAVENPORT.

IN the old days (a custom laid
    aside
   With breeches and cocked hats)
    the people sent
Their wisest men to make the public laws.
And so, from a brown homestead, where
    the Sound
Drinks the small tribute of the Mianas,
Waved over by the woods of Rippowams,
And hallowed by pure lives and tranquil
    deaths,
Stamford sent up to the councils of the
    State
Wisdom and grace in Abraham Daven-
    port.

'T was on a May-day of the far old year
Seventeen hundred eighty, that there fell
Over the bloom and sweet life of the
      Spring,
Over the fresh earth and the heaven of
      noon,
A horror of great darkness, like the night
In day of which the Norland sagas tell, —
The Twilight of the Gods.   The low-hung
      sky
Was black with ominous clouds, save
      where its rim
Was fringed with a dull glow, like that
      which climbs
The crater's sides from the red hell below.
Birds ceased to sing, and all the barn-
      yard fowls
Roosted ; the cattle at the pasture bars
Lowed, and looked homeward ; bats on
      leathern wings
Flitted abroad ; the sounds of labor died ;
Men prayed, and women wept ; all ears
      grew sharp
To hear the doom-blast of the trumpet
      shatter
The black sky, that the dreadful face of
      Christ

Might look from the rent clouds, not as
    he looked
A loving guest at Bethany, but stern
As Justice and inexorable Law.

    Meanwhile in the old State House, dim
       as ghosts,
Sat the lawgivers of Connecticut,
Trembling beneath their legislative robes.
" It is the Lord's Great Day ! Let us ad-
    journ,"
Some said ; and then, as if with one ac-
    cord,
All eyes were turned to Abraham Daven-
    port.
He rose, slow cleaving with his steady
    voice
The intolerable hush. " This well may be
The Day of Judgment which the world
    awaits ;
But be it so or not, I only know
My present duty, and my Lord's com-
    mand
To occupy till He come. So at the post
Where He hath set me in His providence,
I choose, for one, to meet Him face to
    face, —

No faithless servant frightened from my
    task,
But ready when the Lord of the harvest
    calls ;
And therefore, with all reverence, I would
    say,
Let God do His work, we will see to ours.
Bring in the candles." And they brought
    them in.

Then by the flaring lights the Speaker
    read,
Albeit with husky voice and shaking hands,
An act to amend an act to regulate
The shad and alewive fisheries. Where-
    upon
Wisely and well spake Abraham Daven-
    port,
Straight to the question, with no figures
    of speech
Save the ten Arab signs, yet not without
The shrewd dry humor natural to the
    man :
His awe-struck colleagues listening all the
    while,
Between the pauses of his argument,

To hear the thunder of the wrath of God
Break from the hollow trumpet of the
cloud.

And there he stands in memory to this
day,
Erect, self-poised, a rugged face, half seen
Against the background of unnatural dark,
A witness to the ages as they pass,
That simple duty hath no place for fear.

NAUHAUGHT, THE DEACON.

NAUHAUGHT, the Indian deacon,
who of old
Dwelt, poor but blameless, where
his narrowing Cape
Stretches its shrunk arm out to all the
winds
And the relentless smiting of the waves,
Awoke one morning from a pleasant
dream
Of a good angel dropping in his hand
A fair, broad gold-piece, in the name of
God.

He rose and went forth with the early day
Far inland, where the voices of the waves
Mellowed and mingled with the whispering
    leaves,
As, through the tangle of the low, thick
    woods,
He searched his traps. Therein nor
    beast nor bird
He found; though meanwhile in the
    reedy pools
The otter plashed, and underneath the
    pines
The partridge drummed: and as his
    thoughts went back
To the sick wife and little child at home,
What marvel that the poor man felt his
    faith
Too weak to bear its burden, — like a
    rope
That, strand by strand uncoiling, breaks
    above
The hand that grasps it. "Even now, O
    Lord!
Send me," he prayed, "the angel of my
    dream!
Nauhaught is very poor; he cannot wait."

Even as he spake he heard at his bare feet

A low, metallic clink, and, looking down,
He saw a dainty purse with disks of gold
Crowding its silken net.   Awhile he held
The treasure up before his eyes, alone
With his great need, feeling the wondrous
    coins
Slide through his eager fingers, one by
    one.
So then the dream was true.   The angel
    brought
One broad piece only; should he take all
    these ?
Who would be wiser, in the blind, dumb
    woods ?
The loser, doubtless rich, would scarcely
    miss
This dropped crumb from a table always
    full.
Still, while he mused, he seemed to hear
    the cry
Of a starved child ; the sick face of his
    wife
Tempted him.   Heart and flesh in fierce
    revolt
Urged the wild license of his savage youth
Against his later scruples.   Bitter toil,
Prayer, fasting, dread of blame, and piti-
    less eyes

To watch his halting, — had he lost for
      these
The freedom of the woods ; — the hunting-
      grounds
Of happy spirits for a walled-in heaven
Of everlasting psalms ?   One healed the
      sick
Very far off thousands of moons ago :
Had he not prayed him night and day to
      come
And cure his bed-bound wife ?   Was
      there a hell ?
Were all his fathers' people writhing
      there —
Like the poor shell-fish set to boil alive —
Forever, dying never ?   If he kept
This gold, so needed, would the dreadful
      God
Torment him like a Mohawk's captive
      stuck
With slow-consuming splinters ?   Would
      the saints
And the white angels dance and laugh to
      see him
Burn like a pitch-pine torch ?   His Chris-
      tian garb
Seemed falling from him ; with the fear
      and shame

Of Adam naked at the cool of day,
He gazed around. A black snake lay in
    coil
On the hot sand, a crow with sidelong
    eye
Watched from a dead bough. All his In-
    dian lore
Of evil blending with a convert's faith
In the supernal terrors of the Book,
He saw the Tempter in the coiling snake
And ominous, black-winged bird ; and all
    the while
The low rebuking of the distant waves
Stole in upon him like the voice of God
Among the trees of Eden. Girding up
His soul's loins with a resolute hand, he
    thrust
The base thought from him : " Nauhaught,
    be a man !
Starve, if need be ; but, while you live,
    look out
From honest eyes on all men, unashamed.
God help me ! I am deacon of the church,
A baptized, praying Indian ! Should I do
This secret meanness, even the barken
    knots
Of the old trees would turn to eyes to
    see it,

The birds would tell of it, and all the
    leaves
Whisper above me: 'Nauhaught is a
    thief!'
The sun would know it, and the stars that
    hide
Behind his light would watch me, and at
    night
Follow me with their sharp, accusing eyes.
Yea, thou, God, seest me!" Then Nau-
    haught drew
Closer his belt of leather, dulling thus
The pain of hunger, and walked bravely
    back
To the brown fishing-hamlet by the sea;
And, pausing at the inn-door, cheerily
    asked:
"Who hath lost aught to-day?"
                 "I," said a voice;
"Ten golden pieces, in a silken purse,
My daughter's handiwork." He looked,
    and lo!
One stood before him in a coat of frieze,
And the glazed hat of a seafaring man,
Shrewd-faced, broad-shouldered, with no
    trace of wings.
Marvelling, he dropped within the stran-
    ger's hand

The silken web, and turned to go his way.
But the man said: "A tithe at least is
　　yours ;
Take it in God's name as an honest man."
And as the deacon's dusky fingers closed
Over the golden gift, "Yea, in God's name
I take it, with a poor man's thanks," he
　　said.

So down the street that, like a river of
　　sand,
Ran, white in sunshine, to the summer sea,
He sought his home, singing and praising
　　God ;
And when his neighbors in their careless
　　way
Spoke of the owner of the silken purse —
A Wellfleet skipper, known in every port
That the Cape opens in its sandy wall —
He answered, with a wise smile, to him-
　　self :
"I saw the angel where they see a man."

IN SCHOOL-DAYS.

STILL sits the school-house by the
  road,
  A ragged beggar sleeping ;
Around it still the sumachs grow,
  And blackberry-vines are creeping.

Within, the master's desk is seen,
  Deep scarred by raps official ;
The warping floor, the battered seats,
  The jack-knife's carved initial ;

The charcoal frescos on its wall ;
  Its door's worn sill, betraying
The feet that, creeping slow to school,
  Went storming out to playing !

Long years ago a winter sun
  Shone over it at setting ;
Lit up its western window-panes,
  And low eaves' icy fretting.

It touched the tangled golden curls,
  And brown eyes full of grieving,

Of one who still her steps delayed
   When all the school were leaving.

For near her stood the little boy
   Her childish favor singled :
His cap pulled low upon a face
   Where pride and shame were mingled.

Pushing with restless feet the snow
   To right and left, he lingered ; —
As restlessly her tiny hands
   The blue-checked apron fingered.

He saw her lift her eyes ; he felt
   The soft hand's light caressing,
And heard the tremble of her voice,
   As if a fault confessing.

" I 'm sorry that I spelt the word :
   I hate to go above you,
Because," — the brown eyes lower fell, —
   " Because you see, I love you ! "

Still memory to a gray-haired man
   That sweet child-face is showing.
Dear girl ! the grasses on her grave
   Have forty years been growing !

He lives to learn, in life's hard school,
How few who pass above him
Lament their triumph and his loss,
Like her, — because they love him.

SUNSET ON THE BEARCAMP.

GOLD fringe on the purpling
hem
Of hills the river runs,
As down its long, green valley falls
The last of summer's suns.
Along its tawny gravel-bed
Broad-flowing, swift, and still,
As if its meadow levels felt
The hurry of the hill,
Noiseless between its banks of green
From curve to curve it slips ;
The drowsy maple-shadows rest
Like fingers on its lips.

A waif from Carroll's wildest hills,
Unstoried and unknown ;
The ursine legend of its name
Prowls on its banks alone.

Yet flowers as fair its slopes adorn
   As ever Yarrow knew,
Or, under rainy Irish skies,
   By Spenser's Mulla grew ;
And through the gaps of leaning trees
   Its mountain cradle shows :
The gold against the amethyst,
   The green against the rose.

Touched by a light that hath no name,
   A glory never sung,
Aloft on sky and mountain wall
   Are God's great pictures hung.
How changed the summits vast and
     old !
   No longer granite-browed,
They melt in rosy mist ; the rock
   Is softer than the cloud ;
The valley holds its breath ; no leaf
   Of all its elms is twirled :
The silence of eternity
   Seems falling on the world.

The pause before the breaking seals
   Of mystery is this ;
Yon miracle-play of night and day
   Makes dumb its witnesses.

What unseen altar crowns the hills
  That reach up stair on stair?
What eyes look through, what white wings
    fan
  These purple veils of air?
What Presence from the heavenly heights
  To those of earth stoops down?
Not vainly Hellas dreamed of gods
  On Ida's snowy crown!

Slow fades the vision of the sky,
  The golden water pales,
And over all the valley-land
  A gray-winged vapor sails.
I go the common way of all;
  The sunset fires will burn,
The flowers will blow, the river flow,
  When I no more return.
No whisper from the mountain pine
  Nor lapsing stream shall tell
The stranger, treading where I tread,
  Of him who loved them well.

But beauty seen is never lost,
  God's colors all are fast;
The glory of this sunset heaven
  Into my soul has passed,

A sense of gladness unconfined
  To mortal date or clime ;
As the soul liveth, it shall live
  Beyond the years of time.
Beside the mystic asphodels
  Shall bloom the home-born flowers,
And new horizons flush and glow
  With sunset hues of ours.

Farewell ! these smiling hills must wear
  Too soon their wintry frown,
And snow-cold winds from off them shake
  The maple's red leaves down.
But I shall see a summer sun
  Still setting broad and low ;
The mountain slopes shall blush and
     bloom,
  The golden water flow.
A lover's claim is mine on all
  I see to have and hold, —
The rose-light of perpetual hills,
  And sunsets never cold !

WILLIAM FRANCIS BARTLETT.

H, well may Essex sit forlorn
  Beside her sea-blown shore ;
 Her well beloved, her noblest
   born,
 Is hers in life no more !

No lapse of years can render less
 Her memory's sacred claim ;
No fountain of forgetfulness
 Can wet the lips of Fame.

A grief alike to wound and heal,
 A thought to soothe and pain,
The sad, sweet pride that mothers feel
 To her must still remain.

Good men and true she has not lacked,
 And brave men yet shall be ;
The perfect flower, the crowning fact,
 Of all her years was he !

As Galahad pure, as Merlin sage,
 What worthier knight was found
To grace in Arthur's golden age
 The fabled Table Round ?

A voice, the battle's trumpet-note,
  To welcome and restore ;
A hand, that all unwilling smote,
  To heal and build once more !

A soul of fire, a tender heart
  Too warm for hate, he knew
The generous victor's graceful part
  To sheathe the sword he drew.

When Earth, as if on evil dreams,
  Looks back upon her wars,
And the white light of Christ outstreams
  From the red disk of Mars,

His fame who led the stormy van
  Of battle well may cease,
But never that which crowns the man
  Whose victory was Peace.

Mourn, Essex, on thy sea-blown shore
  Thy beautiful and brave,
Whose failing hand the olive bore,
  Whose dying lips forgave !

Let age lament the youthful chief,
  And tender eyes be dim ;

The tears are more of joy than grief
  That fall for one like him !

THE HENCHMAN.

M Y lady walks her morning round,
  My lady's page her fleet grey-
      hound,
My lady's hair the fond winds stir,
And all the birds make songs for her.

Her thrushes sing in Rathburn bowers,
And Rathburn side is gay with flowers ;
But ne'er like hers, in flower or bird,
Was beauty seen or music heard.

The distance of the stars is hers ;
The least of all her worshippers,
The dust beneath her dainty heel,
She knows not that I see or feel.

Oh, proud and calm ! — she cannot know
Where'er she goes with her I go ;

Oh, cold and fair ! — she cannot guess
I kneel to share her hound's caress !

Gay knights beside her hunt and hawk,
I rob their ears of her sweet talk ;
Her suitors come from east and west,
I steal her smiles from every guest.

Unheard of her, in loving words,
I greet her with the song of birds ;
I reach her with her green-armed bowers,
I kiss her with the lips of flowers.

The hound and I are on her trail,
The wind and I uplift her veil ;
As if the calm, cold moon she were,
And I the tide, I follow her.

As unrebuked as they, I share
The license of the sun and air,
And in a common homage hide
My worship from her scorn and pride.

World-wide apart, and yet so near,
I breathe her charmëd atmosphere,
Wherein to her my service brings
The reverence due to holy things.

Her maiden pride, her haughty name,
My dumb devotion shall not shame;
The love that no return doth crave
To knightly levels lifts the slave.

No lance have I, in joust or fight,
To splinter in my lady's sight;
But, at her feet, how blest were I
For any need of hers to die!

THE BAY OF SEVEN ISLANDS.

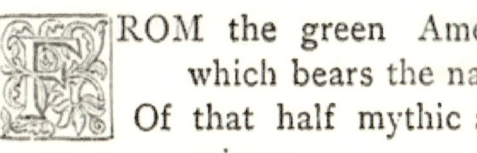

ROM the green Amesbury hill
      which bears the name
   Of that half mythic ancestor of
      mine
Who trod its slopes two hundred years
      ago,
Down the long valley of the Merrimac,
Midway between me and the river's mouth,
I see thy home, set like an eagle's nest
Among Deer Island's immemorial pines,
Crowning the crag on which the sunset
      breaks

Its last red arrow.   Many a tale and song,
Which thou hast told or sung, I call to
    mind,
Softening with silvery mist the woods and
    hills,
The out-thrust headlands and inreaching
    bays
Of our northeastern coast-line, trending
    where
The Gulf, midsummer, feels the chill
    blockade
Of icebergs stranded at its northern gate.

To thee the echoes of the Island Sound
Answer not vainly, nor in vain the moan
Of the South Breaker prophesying storm.
And thou hast listened, like myself, to
    men
Sea-periled oft where Anticosti lies
Like a fell spider in its web of fog,
Or where the Grand Bank shallows with
    the wrecks   .
Of sunken fishers, and to whom strange
    isles
And frost-rimmed bays and trading sta-
    tions seem
Familiar as Great Neck and Kettle Cove,

Nubble and Boon, the common names of
     home.
So let me offer thee this lay of mine,
Simple and homely, lacking much thy play
Of color and of fancy.   If its theme
And   treatment   seem   to thee befitting
     youth
Rather than age, let this be my excuse :
It has beguiled some heavy hours and
     called
Some pleasant memories up ; and, better
     still,
Occasion lent me for a kindly word
To one who is my neighbor and my friend.

The skipper sailed out of the harbor
     mouth,
Leaving the apple-bloom of the South
    For the ice of the Eastern seas,
    In his fishing schooner Breeze.

Handsome and brave and young was he,
And the maids of Newbury sighed to see
    His lessening white sail fall
    Under the sea's blue wall.

Through the Northern Gulf and the misty
 screen
Of the isles of Mingan and Madeleine,
 St. Paul's and Blanc Sablon,
 The little Breeze sailed on,

Backward and forward, along the shore
Of lorn and desolate Labrador,
 And found at last her way
 To the Seven Islands Bay.

The little hamlet, nestling below
Great hills white with lingering snow,
 With its tin-roofed chapel stood
 Half hid in the dwarf spruce wood ;

Green-turfed, flower-sown, the last outpost
Of summer upon the dreary coast,
 With its gardens small and spare,
 Sad in the frosty air.

Hard by where the skipper's schooner lay,
A fisherman's cottage looked away
 Over isle and bay, and behind
 On mountains dim-defined.

And there twin sisters, fair and young,
Laughed with their stranger guest, and sung

In their native tongue the lays
Of the old Provençal days.

Alike were they, save the faint outline
Of a scar on Suzette's forehead fine ;
    And both, it so befell,
    Loved the heretic stranger well.

Both were pleasant to look upon,
But the heart of the skipper clave to one ;
    Though less by his eye than heart
    He knew the twain apart.

Despite of alien race and creed,
Well did his wooing of Marguerite speed ;
    And the mother's wrath was vain
    As the sister's jealous pain.

The shrill-tongued mistress her house for-
        bade,
And solemn warning was sternly said
    By the black-robed priest, whose word
    As law the hamlet heard.

But half by voice and half by signs
The skipper said, " A warm sun shines
    On the green-banked Merrimac ;
    Wait, watch, till I come back.

" And when you see, from my mast head,
The signal fly of a kerchief red,
    My boat on the shore shall wait ;
    Come, when the night is late."

Ah ! weighed with childhood's haunts and
    friends,
And all that the home sky overbends,
    Did ever young love fail
    To turn the trembling scale ?

Under the night, on the wet sea sands,
Slowly unclasped their plighted hands :
    One to the cottage hearth,
    And one to his sailor's berth.

What was it the parting lovers heard ?
Nor leaf, nor ripple, nor wing of bird,
    But a listener's stealthy tread
    On the rock-moss, crisp and dead.

He weighed his anchor, and fished once
    more
By the black coast-line of Labrador ;
    And by love and the north wind
    driven,
    Sailed back to the Islands Seven.

In the sunset's glow the sisters twain
Saw the Breeze come sailing in again ;
 Said Suzette, " Mother dear,
 The heretic's sail is here."

" Go, Marguerite, to your room, and hide ;
Your door shall be bolted!" the mother
  cried :
 While Suzette, ill at ease,
 Watched the red sign of the Breeze.

At midnight, down to the waiting skiff
She stole in the shadow of the cliff ;
 And out of the Bay's mouth ran
 The schooner with maid and man.

And all night long, on a restless bed,
Her prayers to the Virgin Marguerite said :
 And thought of her lover's pain
 Waiting for her in vain.

Did he pace the sands ?   Did he pause to
  hear
The sound of her light step drawing near ?
 And, as the slow hours passed,
 Would he doubt her faith at last ?

But when she saw through the misty
      pane
The morning break on a sea of rain,
      Could even her love avail
      To follow his vanished sail?

Meantime the Breeze, with favoring wind,
Left the rugged Moisic hills behind,
      And heard from an unseen shore
      The falls of Manitou roar.

On the morrow's morn, in the thick, gray
      weather
They sat on the reeling deck together,
      Lover and counterfeit
      Of hapless Marguerite.

With a lover's hand, from her forehead
      fair
He smoothed away her jet-black hair.
      What was it his fond eyes met?
      The scar of the false Suzette!

Fiercely he shouted : " Bear away
East by north for Seven Isles Bay!"
      The maiden wept and prayed,
      But the ship her helm obeyed.

Once more the Bay of the Isles they
    found :
They heard the bell of the chapel sound,
    And the chant of the dying sung
    In the harsh, wild Indian tongue.

A feeling of mystery, change, and awe
Was in all they heard and all they saw :
    Spell-bound the hamlet lay
    In the hush of its lonely bay.

And when they came to the cottage door,
The mother rose up from her weeping
    sore,
    And with angry gestures met
    The scared look of Suzette.

"Here is your daughter," the skipper
    said ;
" Give me the one I love instead."
    But the woman sternly spake ;
    "Go, see if the dead will wake ! "

He looked.   Her sweet face still and
    white
And strange in the noonday taper light,
    She lay on her little bed,
    With the cross at her feet and head.

In a passion of grief the strong man
    bent
Down to her face, and, kissing it, went
      Back to the waiting Breeze,
      Back to the mournful seas.

Never again to the Merrimac
And Newbury's homes that bark came
    back.
      Whether her fate she met
      On the shores of Carraquette,

Miscou, or Tracadie, who can say?
But even yet at Seven Isles Bay
      Is told the ghostly tale
      Of a weird, unspoken sail,

In the pale, sad light of the Northern day
Seen by the blanketed Montagnais,
      Or squaw, in her small kyack,
      Crossing the spectre's track.

On the deck a maiden wrings her hands;
Her likeness kneels on the gray coast
    sands;
      One in her wild despair,
      And one in the trance of prayer.

She flits before no earthly blast,
The red sign fluttering from her mast,
    Over the solemn seas,
    The ghost of the schooner Breeze !

ICHABOD.

1850.

O fallen ! so lost ! the light with-
    drawn
    Which once he wore !
The glory from his gray hairs gone
    Forevermore !

Revile him not, the Tempter hath
    A snare for all ;
And pitying tears, not scorn and wrath,
    Befit his fall !

Oh, dumb be passion's stormy rage,
    When he who might
Have lighted up and led his age
    Falls back in night.

Scorn ! would the angels laugh, to mark
     A bright soul driven,
Fiend-goaded, down the endless dark,
     From hope and heaven !

Let not the land once proud of him
     Insult him now,
Nor brand with deeper shame his dim,
     Dishonored brow.

But let its humbled sons, instead,
     From sea to lake,
A long lament, as for the dead,
     In sadness make.

Of all we loved and honored, naught
     Save power remains ;
A fallen angel's pride of thought,
     Still strong in chains.

All else is gone ; from those great eyes
     The soul has fled :
When faith is lost, when honor dies
     The man is dead !

Then, pay the reverence of old days
     To his dead fame ;

Walk backward, with averted gaze,
And hide his shame !

THE LOST OCCASION.

1880.

OME die too late and some too
soon,
At early morning, heat of noon,
Or the chill evening twilight.   Thou,
Whom the rich heavens did so endow
With eyes of power and Jove's own brow,
With all the massive strength that fills
Thy home-horizon's granite hills,
With rarest gifts of heart and head
From manliest stock inherited,
New England's stateliest type of man,
In port and speech Olympian ;
Whom no one met, at first, but took
A second awed and wondering look
(As turned, perchance, the eyes of Greece
On Phidias' unveiled masterpiece) ;
Whose words, in simplest homespun clad,

The Saxon strength of Caedmon's had,
With power reserved at need to reach
The Roman forum's loftiest speech,
Sweet with persuasion, eloquent
In passion, cool in argument,
Or, ponderous, falling on thy foes
As fell the Norse god's hammer blows,
Crushing as with Talus' flail
Through Error's logic-woven mail,
And failing only when they tried
The adamant of the righteous side, —
Thou, foiled in aim and hope, bereaved
Of old friends, by the new deceived,
Too soon for us, too soon for thee,
Beside thy lonely Northern sea,
Where long and low the marsh-lands
          spread,
Laid wearily down thy august head.

Thou shouldst have lived to feel below
Thy feet Disunion's fierce upthrow;
The late-sprung mine that underlaid
Thy sad concessions vainly made.
Thou shouldst have seen from Sumter's
          wall
The star-flag of the Union fall
And armed rebellion pressing on

The broken lines of Washington !
No stronger voice than thine had then
Called out the utmost might of men,
To make the Union's charter free
And strengthen law by liberty.
How had that stern arbitrament
To thy gray age youth's vigor lent,
Shaming ambition's paltry prize
Before thy disillusioned eyes ;
Breaking the spell about thee wound
Like the green withes that Samson bound ;
Redeeming, in one effort grand,
Thyself and thy imperilled land !
Ah, cruel fate, that closed to thee,
O sleeper by the Northern sea,
The gates of opportunity !
God fills the gaps of human need,
Each crisis brings its word and deed.
Wise men and strong we did not lack ;
But still, with memory turning back,
In the dark hours we thought of thee,
And thy lone grave beside the sea.

Above that grave the east winds blow,
And from the marsh-lands drifting slow
The sea-fog comes, with evermore
The wave-wash of a lonely shore,

And sea-bird's melancholy cry,
As Nature fain would typify
The sadness of a closing scene,
The loss of that which should have been.
But where thy native mountains bare
Their foreheads to diviner air,
Fit emblem of enduring fame,
One lofty summit keeps thy name.
For thee, the cosmic forces did
The rearing of that pyramid,
The prescient ages shaping with
Fire, flood, and frost thy monolith.
Sunrise and sunset lay thereon
With hands of light their benison,
The stars of midnight pause to set
Their jewels in its coronet.
And evermore that mountain mass
Seems climbing from the shadowy pass
To light, as if to manifest
Thy nobler self, thy life at best!

STORM ON LAKE ASQUAM.

CLOUD, like that the old-time
      Hebrew saw
  On Carmel prophesying rain,
    began
To lift itself o'er wooded Cardigan,
Growing and blackening. Suddenly, a
  flaw

Of chill wind menaced; then a strong
    blast beat
  Down the long valley's murmuring pines,
    and woke
  The noon-dream of the sleeping lake,
    and broke
Its smooth steel mirror at the mountains'
  feet.

Thunderous and vast, a fire-veined dark-
    ness swept
  Over the rough pine-bearded Asquam
    range;
  A wraith of tempest, wonderful and
    strange,
From peak to peak the cloudy giant
  stepped.

One moment, as if challenging the storm,
   Chocorua's tall, defiant sentinel
   Looked from his watch-tower ; then the
      shadow fell,
And the wild rain-drift blotted out his
      form.

And over all the still unhidden sun,
   Weaving its light through slant-blown
      veils of rain,
   Smiled on the trouble, as hope smiles
      on pain ;
And, when the tumult and the strife were
      done,

With one foot on the lake and one on
      land,
   Framing within his crescent's tinted
      streak
   A far-off picture of the Melvin peak,
Spent broken clouds the rainbow's angel
      spanned.

BIRCHBROOK MILL.

 NOTELESS stream, the Birch-
brook runs
Beneath its leaning trees ;
That low, soft ripple is its own,
That dull roar is the sea's.

Of human signs it sees alone
The distant church spire's tip,
And, ghost-like, on a blank of gray,
The white sail of a ship.

No more a toiler at the wheel,
It wanders at its will ;
Nor dam nor pond is left to tell
Where once was Birchbrook mill.

The timbers of that mill have fed
Long since a farmer's fires ;
His doorsteps are the stones that ground
The harvest of his sires.

Man trespassed here ; but Nature lost
No right of her domain ;
She waited, and she brought the old
Wild beauty back again.

By day the sunlight through the leaves
    Falls on its moist, green sod,
And wakes the violet bloom of spring
    And autumn's golden-rod.

Its birches whisper to the wind,
    The swallow dips her wings
In the cool spray, and on its banks
    The gray song-sparrow sings.

But from it, when the dark night falls,
    The school-girl shrinks with dread ;
The farmer, home-bound from his fields,
    Goes by with quickened tread.

They dare not pause to hear the grind
    Of shadowy stone on stone ;
The plashing of a water-wheel
    Where wheel there now is none.

Has not a cry of pain been heard
    Above the clattering mill?
The pawing of an unseen horse,
    Who waits his mistress still?

Yet never to the listener's eye
    Has sight confirmed the sound ;

A wavering birch line marks alone
   The vacant pasture ground.

No ghostly arms fling up to heaven
   The agony of prayer ;
No spectral steed impatient shakes
   His white mane on the air.

The meaning of that common dread
   No tongue has fitly told ;
The secret of the dark surmise
   The brook and birches hold.

What nameless horror of the past
   Broods here forevermore ?
What ghost his unforgiven sin
   Is grinding o'er and o'er?

Does, then, immortal memory play
   The actor's tragic part,
Rehearsals of a mortal life
   And unveiled human heart ?

God's pity spare a guilty soul
   That drama of its ill,
And let the scenic curtain fall
   On Birchbrook's haunted mill !

THE BARTHOLDI STATUE.

THE land, that, from the rule of
   kings,
     In freeing us, itself made free,
Our Old World Sister, to us brings
   Her sculptured Dream of Liberty :

Unlike the shapes on Egypt's sands,
   Uplifted by the toil-worn slave,
On Freedom's soil with freemen's hands
   We rear the symbol free hands gave.

O France, the beautiful ! to thee
   Once more a debt of love we owe :
In peace beneath thy Colors Three,
   We hail a later Rochambeau !

Rise, stately Symbol ! holding forth
   Thy light and hope to all who sit
In chains and darkness !   Belt the earth
   With watch-fires from thy torch uplit !

Reveal the primal mandate still
   Which Chaos heard and ceased to be,

Trace on mid-air th' Eternal Will
　　In signs of fire : " Let man be free ! "

Shine far, shine free, a guiding light
　　To Reason's ways and Virtue's aim,
A lightning-flash the wretch to smite
　　Who shields his license with thy name !

AT LAST.

HEN on my day of life the night
　　　　is falling,
　　　　And, in the winds from un-
　　　　sunned spaces blown,
I hear far voices out of darkness calling
　　My feet to paths unknown,

Thou who hast made my home of life so
　　　　pleasant,
　　Leave not its tenant when its walls de-
　　　　cay ;
O Love Divine, O Helper ever present,
　　Be Thou my strength and stay !

Be near me when all else is from me drift-
　　ing:
　Earth, sky, home's pictures, days of
　　shade and shine,
And kindly faces to my own uplifting
　The love which answers mine.

I have but Thee, my Father! let Thy
　　spirit
　Be with me then to comfort and uphold;
No gate of pearl, no branch of palm I merit,
　Nor street of shining gold.

Suffice it if — my good and ill unreck-
　　oned,
　And both forgiven through Thy abound-
　　ing grace —
I find myself by hands familiar beckoned
　Unto my fitting place.

Some humble door among Thy many
　　mansions,
　Some sheltering shade where sin and
　　striving cease,
And flows forever through heaven's green
　　expansions
　The river of Thy peace.

There, from the music round about me
    stealing,
  I fain would learn the new and holy
    song,
And find at last, beneath Thy trees of
    healing,
  The life for which I long.

WHITTIER'S WORKS.

POEMS. Cabinet Edition. 16mo, $1.00.
Household Edition. With Portrait. 12mo, $1.50; full gilt,
$2.00.
Family Edition. Illustrated. 8vo, full gilt, $2.50.
Illustrated Library Edition. With Portrait and Illustrations.
8vo, full gilt, $3.00.

POETICAL WORKS. Riverside Edition. 4 vols. crown
8vo, gilt top, $6.00.

PROSE WORKS. Riverside Edition. 3 vols. crown 8vo,
gilt top, $4.50.

COMPLETE WORKS. Riverside Edition. 7 vols.
crown 8vo, gilt top, $10.50.

EARLY POEMS. 12mo, full gilt, $1.00.

THE VISION OF ECHARD, AND OTHER POEMS.
16mo, gilt top, $1.25.

SNOW-BOUND. 16mo, $1.00.
Illustrated Edition. With 40 Illustrations. 8vo, flexible
leather, $2.00.

MAUD MULLER. With Illustrations. 8vo, full gilt,
$2.50.

BALLADS OF NEW ENGLAND. With 60 Illustrations. 8vo, flexible leather, $2.00.

MABEL MARTIN With 58 Illustrations. 8vo, full gilt,
$2.00.
Popular Edition. Illustrated. 16mo, $1.50.

THE KING'S MISSIVE. With Portrait. 16mo, gilt
top, $1.00.

THE BAY OF SEVEN ISLANDS. With Portrait.
16mo, gilt top, $1.00.

POEMS OF NATURE. With Illustrations. Quarto, full
gilt, $6.00.

ST. GREGORY'S GUEST, AND RECENT POEMS.
16mo, illuminated vellum covers, $1.00.

LEGENDS AND LYRICS. From Whittier. In White
and Gold Series. 16mo, $1.00.

CHILD LIFE. Edited by Whittier. Illustrated. 12mo,
full gilt, $2.00.

CHILD LIFE IN PROSE. Edited by Whittier. Illustrated. 12mo, full gilt, $2.00.

**SONGS OF THREE CENTURIES. Household Edi-
tion.** 12mo, $1.50; full gilt, $2.00.
Illustrated Library Edition. 8vo, full gilt, $3.00.

HOUGHTON, MIFFLIN & CO.
BOSTON AND NEW YORK.